BOOK ONE
MOTHER • MAIDEN • CRONE

BY CULLEN BUNN

Created, managed, and written by Cullen Bunn for the Outer Shadows Imprint.

Visit outershadows.org to see more.

Published by Outland Entertainment LLC
3119 Gillham Road
Kansas City, MO 64109

Publisher: Jeremy D. Mohler
Editor-in-Chief: Alana Joli Abbott
Chief Creative Officer: Anton Kromoff

ISBN: 978-1-954255-73-9
EBOOK ISBN: 978-1-954255-74-6
Worldwide Rights
Created in the United States of America

Editor: Scott Colby
Cover Illustration: Baldemar Rivas
Logo Design: Viktor Farro
Cover & Interior Design: Jeremy D. Mohler

Printed and bound in the United States of America.

Visit outlandentertainment.com to see more, or follow us on our Facebook Page facebook.com/outlandentertainment/.

RAZE CREATED BY CULLEN BUNN & SHAWN LEE

ONE

After a time, she knew only screaming.

There was pain, yes, flowing through her body, her nerves afire with its passing. It washed across her—washed *through* her—like smashing tidal waves of agony crashing upon black shores, then rushing back into the boundless darkness—an endless sea of misery and suffering waiting to be plumbed—only to crash over her once again, stronger and more violent with each subsequent visitation. But it was not the pain that brought a sharp cry to her soft lips.

The pain...constant as the torture continued, constant as cruel hands mistreated her flesh, constant as blood was coaxed from her veins...was a companion. A friend. The pain was familiar even in these unfamiliar circumstances.

With the pain came assurance.

I am still alive.

With the pain came promise.

I will heal.

But under the relentless scrutiny of her captor's ministrations, even the constant of pain, within which she had taken solace, had abandoned her. The agony withered from familiarity, becoming commonplace. She no longer felt the searing hot needles as they lanced through her skin, piercing her, digging deep, burrowing into bone.

The pain faded.

Until she felt nothing at all.

And so she screamed.

TWO

Three nights earlier.

Against a sky of black and crimson stood the Convent of the Sacred Visitation. Once, centuries ago, the stoic structure had been a silent sentinel at the foothills of a great mountain pass. But the Anderhalls had been beaten down over time, blasted to rubble during the fierce battles of the ages-long Gilgorom Faith Wars and ground to dust when the Valgerai, in a bold assault on the nation of Ambercast, led an army of mammoth-riders through the Narrow Reach.

That the convent had survived these countless, brutal conflicts and conquests was a testament to the structure's defenses and to the purpose of the holy order which called the place home. The high, stark walls of thick stone, raised by a now-forgotten warlord during the Second Age, were the envy of many dethroned kings weeping in the rubble of their demolished fortress. And while some military strategists believed the convent could withstand the assault of ten-thousand men, it was the order's mission, not its might, which afforded the Sisterhood the greatest sense of safety and protection.

Founded by Saint Desmiel the Healer, the Sisterhood of the Sacred Visitation were hospitallers, and they were sworn, as was the edict of their patron, to turn no injured man away—regardless of his creed, code, or religion. The wounded, the sick, the dying—all found warmth and care beyond the convent's gates. The Sisterhood asked for nothing in return save that battle and bloodshed be forgotten within this place of healing. No warmonger, no matter how bloodthirsty, could overlook the value of such a resource.

And so the Sisterhood knew peace in a time of unending war.

Matron Clarissa gazed from her chamber's window across the vast expanse of war-ravaged wasteland that served as the convent's promenade. In the distance, columns of black smoke uncurled into the darkening sky. Flames could be seen along the already bloody horizon.

"Another battle," Clarissa muttered. "Who is it this time?"

Behind her, sitting upon a stool in the corner, Anna stirred.

"In my dreams, I saw two beasts locked in a struggle of life and death," the young girl said. "The viper wrapped itself around the hawk's neck, but the hawk buried its talons in the serpent's belly. The two of them spun into the air as if caught in a violent wind, then plummeted to the earth to be dashed, the both of them, upon the rocks."

Clarissa considered the girl's words for a moment, then nodded, more to herself than to anyone.

"The armies of Fellwind carry the banner of the hawk, and the forces of Xendraken are represented by the serpent. Lords Grevely and Rajenva are at it again. We should make ready. Our beds will be filled with the wounded and dying before the night is done."

She turned away from the window and faced Anna. Even now, after months in the acolyte's presence, Clarissa found herself taken aback by the girl's beauty. Not only her beauty, but her purity. The girl was but sixteen winters old, and she had been rescued by the convent from what would have surely been the life of a concubine. Clothed from head to toe in the white and sky-blue robes of a nescient servant of Saint Desmiel, she was the very definition of magnificence, with her high cheekbones, perfectly-formed lips, ocean-deep eyes, and golden hair. Many of the Sisterhood were secretly envious of the girl, the Matron knew, not only for her natural loveliness, but for the favor Clarissa bestowed upon her. Even the Matron, who had served Desmiel's order for twenty years (and was herself a striking woman) was not immune to petty jealousies. At times, she found herself longing for the girl's youth and vitality and innocence, for in her innocence and virtue, Anna had been blessed by Saint Desmiel.

"There is something more," Anna said. She looked down, afraid to meet Clarissa's gaze.

The Matron crossed the room and touched two fingers to the girl's chin. She raised Anna's head so their eyes might meet. "What is it? What else do you see?"

"I saw our order torn asunder."

"The Sisterhood destroyed?" Clarissa tried to remain calm, to speak coolly and reassuringly. But at times the cryptic nature of the acolyte's rambling grew tiresome. "How could this be?"

"I don't know. I did not see how it came to pass. I only saw our halls littered with the dead."

"We tend fallen soldiers." Clarissa allowed herself the luxury of a slight smile, but the subtle expression of mirth seemed out of place. "We cannot save all of them. Our duty is to give comfort to those who are beyond healing, but in these times, our halls are always filled with the dead."

"I did not dream of dead soldiers." Anna's brow furrowed as if the memory of the dream caused her pain. "I saw the Sisterhood...butchered and drawing flies...bleeding out on the stone floors of the convent... I saw you, Matron Superior, lying among them, staring at me with lifeless eyes...and the flow of blood was only staunched by ashes...ashes filling the halls like a blizzard even though I could discern no flame..."

Matron Clarissa glanced toward her window, her eyes nar-row. Somewhere in the distance, metal rang out against metal. Men called out to one another in the dark. Warriors bellowed their battle cries. The conflict was already spilling into nearby lands. Grevely and Rajenva were old men, too long controlled by their hatred of one another. Could one of them be so consumed by rage that he might strike out at his enemy's only source of solace? Could one of the warlords be planning to attack the Convent of the Sacred Visitation?

"There were figures tending the dead," Anna said, "tending them as surely as the farmer tends his crops. They were wretched, hideous things, twisted and rotting, not on the outside, but within, as if their souls had been corrupted."

"Do you remember anything else?"

"No, Matron Superior." The girl was trembling, and her eyes were sheathed in tears. "But something awful is coming."

A sudden chill danced upon Clarissa's spine. She clenched her hands into fists tight enough to draw blood from her palms. She would not be controlled by doubt and fear.

"That's enough talk of dreams," Clarissa said. "Go tell the others to make ready."

Anna steadied herself, wiped her eyes with the back of her hand, and nodded. She rose from the stool, but she kept her head down, still unwilling to look Matron Clarissa in the eyes.

"Do you still fear the dreams?" Clarissa asked softly.

Still looking at the floor, Anna nodded. "I fear what they show me."

The girl was terrified of the visions, Clarissa knew. At times, she would wake up screaming in the dead of night, and it was not unheard of for Anna to avoid sleep for days on end. Still, she possessed a gift from Desmiel himself, and it would be foolish to squander it, especially in a time of impending strife.

"I am sorry the visions bring you such grief." Clarissa stroked the girl's silky hair. "But I'm afraid I must—"

"No, Matron Superior...please." Anna flinched away. Now the tears came freely, rolling down her cheeks. "Please don't ask me to do this."

Clarissa's face grew stern, her voice sharp.

"I'm *asking* nothing."

Anna looked down again.

"It will take time for the herbs to be prepared," Clarissa said, "but you *will* sleep tonight. You *will* dream."

Anna spoke in a defeated whisper. "Yes, Matron Superior."

As the girl hurried from the chamber, Clarissa detected movement in the darkened hallway beyond her door. She glanced outside and saw a robed figure emerge from the shadows to accompany the acolyte.

Elaynne.

A growl formed in Clarissa's throat.

The bitch was spying on her again, listening right outside her door.

And now, Clarissa thought, *she's pressing Anna for additional details of her dreams, secrets I might have overlooked.*

A few droplets of blood spattered the floor at

Clarissa's feet. She had almost forgotten that she clenched her hands into tight fists. She opened her fingers and looked at her palms. Three crescent cuts were spaced across her two hands. Four crescents, like a calendar counting the moons. Blood oozed from her palms to her wrists, and she clenched her hands closed once more.

Three days.

Perhaps the young virgin was not the only one blessed with portents.

THREE

The cries of the injured echoed through the convent like the wail of the restless dead, and the stone floors of the infirmary were slick with blood. Two of the sisters—younger acolytes who were unaccustomed to the circumstances—had slipped in the gore and twisted their ankles. Already, beds were in short supply, but the casualties continued to flood through the convent's gates.

Anna had tended numerous patients since arriving at the convent. She had seen the men, ripped and mutilated and splayed open, reaching with quivering, bloodied fingers for their nursemaids like helpless infants for their mothers. She had heard them whimpering and mewling and screaming and begging in equal parts for mercy or death.

But…the smell…

She had never grown accustomed to the smell.

The stench was a thick miasma of unwashed and sweaty flesh, copper-tinged blood, urine from voided bladders, and other human waste. One of the men clutched feebly at his stomach, trying to push his own ruptured intestines back into the cavity that had been torn in his belly. The smell oozing from his organs reminded Anna of rotting fowl. Another warrior—a young boy no more than sixteen—had been beaten black and blue, and he vomited repeatedly into his own dented helmet. The helm overflowed, and the reeking, blood-streaked bile spilled down the sides and dribbled into the crimson stew covering the floor.

Anna stood silently at the periphery of the hustle and bustle of the infirmary.

Half-dead men were dragged into the room, many of them being laid on the floor amidst the blood since the number of free beds continued to dwindle. Members of the healing order, their robes sodden with blood and bile and urine and waste, hurried here and there within the massive chamber. They carried clean cloths and buckets of fresh water into the room, and they lugged sanguine rags and buckets filled with blood away. They whispered words of comfort to those who would have them, and they uttered prayers bidding a safe passage to the underworld for those who needed them. Healers called for water and bandages and cutting implements while the dying cried for pity.

Anna found that she could not will her muscles to move nor her eyes to look away.

The patients fell into two distinct classes: the knights of Lord Grevely in their silvered armor and hawk-emblazoned tabards, and the warriors of Lord Rajenva with their heavy beards, calloused hands, and fur and leather armor. Anna wondered what could make these men hate each other so much. But she supposed it did not matter. Here, inside the convent, they were the same.

Another smell filled the air, and Anna's head spun. Several of Anna's sisters entered the chamber, carrying incense braziers. A hazy, pungent smoke poured from the burners, filling the air with the scent of burning herbs and roots the order had harvested from the hillside. In the proper combination, the plants could soothe the body and mind...or when mixed with certain extracts and powders, they could induce sleep and even prophetic dreams in those who were open to such things.

Without realizing it, Anna stepped away from the sisters as they passed, and she held her breath.

She had been ordered back to her chambers to await the drugs for herself. The Matron Superior would be furious if she found that Anna had disobeyed her. But Anna could not stand the thought of drinking the foul potion the Matron's herbalists mixed in their laboratories. The Matron did not understand. How could she? She had not been "blessed" with the gift of foresight. The elixir brought visions, yes, but the visions brought—

Nightmares.

A rough hand grabbed her shoulder. She gasped, spinning.

A large, bearded man leaned against the wall behind her, and as she pulled away, he slipped down into a sitting position. A trail of glistening red marked his descent along the wall. A bloody handprint stained her robes where he had touched her. A half-dozen arrows protruded from his body, the padded animal skins he wore doing little to protect him. He had snapped the fletching away, leaving only the splintered shafts behind. His eyes were wide and desperate, his beard matted. His lips trembled as his mouth worked open and closed.

It took a moment for Anna to recover from her initial shock, but she stepped forward, kneeling beside the man.

"Steady now," she said. "Don't try to talk. I'll...I'll bring you water."

The warrior's eyes rolled around as if he could not quite locate the person speaking to him, then his gaze locked on Anna's and he fixed her with a look of pure terror.

"N-no. No w-water."

"Please," Anna said, clutching at his shoulder. "Be still."

He grabbed her wrist hard enough that she winced in pain. He fingers spasmed open as he pushed her hand away from him.

"Just leave me be." His beard was flecked with frothy spittle. "Leave me be and let me die."

"This...this is a place of healing."

"Not for long." He shook his head weakly. His eyelids fluttered. "Soon it will be a place of *death*."

Anna's breath caught in her throat as the memory of her dream raced through her mind.

"It's coming," the dying man said. "It's coming, and if you're merciful, you'll let me bleed out right here."

"What are you talking about?" Anna looked about

for someone—anyone—who could help her, but the other sisters were all preoccupied with the other wounded. "What's coming?"

"I saw it." He could barely keep his eyes open now. A growing pool of blood spread across the floor around him, oozing into Anna's robes at the knees. "I saw it…in the distance…like a storm slowly stalking us…patient…oh so patient…until it falls upon its prey…"

"I don't understand."

"The flesh-eater," the man muttered.

Anna recoiled from him as if slapped.

And with his last breath, he said, "The Razing."

FOUR

In the bowels of the Convent, the crone stirred.

Withered and grey and cold, she crawled among the darkness.

Among the dust.

Among the secrets.

She could hear the Sisterhood up above, scurrying, tending the dead and the dying.

Without light, without sight, she navigated the vast chamber in which she had been imprisoned. Her clawed fingertips brushed across forgotten swords, loose coins, the desiccated carcasses of rats, the pieces of shattered coffers, human skulls, skeletal remains. Soon, she found the first of many rough-hewn stone steps that led up, up, up through the winding blackness, to an oaken door.

The crone had not seen the door in ages, it seemed, but she knew it was there.

And beyond the door, the wounded, shrieking for solace.

The door, she knew, would be opening soon.

The crone waited.

Her mouth watered.

FIVE

Lightning arced across the sky, and the storm bellowed like a mad giant. The dense foliage provided some cover from the whipping rain and stinging hail, but Siris was already soaked to the bone, and her flesh was dotted with welts. Enswathed in a sodden wool cloak, she felt as if she carried all the weight of the storm upon her shoulders, and yet she knew she had not yet seen the tempest's full fury.

Her hair fell before her eyes, clinging wetly to her face. She wiped the long, dark strands away and looked back the way she had come.

Between the ancient trees, the forest was pitch black. Only when a bolt of jagged lightning set the sky ablaze could Siris see more than a few yards. She had carried a lantern earlier, but it had been doused in the downpour, and she had abandoned it.

The forest floor was a sea of leaves, fallen branches, and dense fungus, broken here and there by islands of unearthed roots. Curtains of damp moss cascaded from crooked branches, and thick, thorny vines drooped low between the trees.

Something *crunched* through the underbrush.

Coming closer.

The storm did little to deter the hungry predators haunting the woods.

In the next flash of lightning, Siris saw four pairs of green, baleful eyes moving through the shadows, approaching cautiously, watching for the right time to strike.

She stood her ground, waiting. She licked the rain from her lips, tasting salt.

Heaven's Tears, her mother had called them.

She hadn't thought of her mother for years. Strange that she would remember her now, as vicious beasts closed in.

Another flash of lightning, and Siris glimpsed four large beasts loping toward her. Wolves, each one larger than a bull mastiff, each one wholly capable of taking down elk on its own.

Of course, Siris thought, *if there were an elk to be found in these woods, they wouldn't bother with the likes of me.*

This was a primordial forest, and few men would set foot in such a place without first making offerings to the gods above and below. Surely, such ancient places were the haven of demons and ghosts. Wolves such as these—man-killers—inspired such legends.

But even legends might starve when game becomes scarce.

As fearsome as the animals might be, they had grown lazy, and they haunted battlefields like common carrion eaters, not as predators. They feasted on fallen soldiers. At least this pack remembered something of their former glory. They had caught the scent of live prey, and their hunter's instincts had kicked in.

More's the pity.

Siris moved backwards, crawling over the trunk of a fallen tree but still keeping her eyes on the dark, hulking shapes stalking her. As she slipped to the other side of the deadfall, she reached into her leather healer's satchel. Her fingers skittered like a spider's legs over the jars of salves, the vials of tonic, the needles, the spools of stitching thread, the bone saw… until at last finding purchase on the implement she sought.

With a snarl, the largest of the pack—the alpha male—leapt upon the fallen tree and glared down upon Siris. Its fur was wet and bristly, and its muzzle and eyes and ears bore the scars of many battles. It bared its fangs, and slobber and rainwater dripped from its snout.

Siris let her satchel fall.

As the bag thumped to the wet ground, the wolf pounced, leaping toward its prey, intent on grabbing her by the throat, bearing her down and snapping her neck. Siris glided to the left, ducking low to avoid the beast, pivoting to draw her right hand—and the scalpel she held—cleanly across the animal's gullet. Lightning flashed again, painting the arc of the creature's blood in stark blacks. The wolf yelped, crashing into the dead leaves and mud.

It trembled and tried to pick itself up, but its throat had been cut to the bone, and its head nearly hung loosely upon its neck. The wolf fell and lay still.

The other three perched like dark gargoyles atop

the dead tree. Snarling, tilting their heads to regard their fallen pack- mate, unable to understand how their prey—their food—had killed the strongest of their number, then turning their gaze toward Siris.

Her shoulders sagged, and the scalpel hung precariously from relaxed fingers. She rolled her own gaze from the dead animal at her feet to the three beasts still salivating at the thought of feasting on her flesh.

The wolves whimpered at the cold intensity of her eyes. One by one, they scampered into the darkness from whence they came. Once they were a safe distance away, they howled mournfully for their leader.

Siris picked up her healer's bag and dropped the scalpel back inside. She nudged the wolf's carcass with the toe of her boot.

"Don't worry," she mused to the dead animal. "Your friends are hungry, and they'll be after a less bothersome meal next time, I think. They'll be back for you soon enough."

She turned away from the wolf and regarded the forest. The old, arboreal sentinels stretched out before her. Somewhere beyond their numbers, out there in the darkness and the rain, stood the Convent of the Sacred Visitation.

How long until she reached its gates?

Another day. Maybe less.

She wondered if the nuns would sense a predator among them.

She wondered if the heavens would weep at what she had planned.

SIX

The bells tolled.

Clarissa surveyed the silvered mirror, and she was pleased with what she saw. She was tall and proud and elegant and fearsome. Her dark hair, only barely touched by the slightest hint of grey, was pulled back beneath the cowl of her station. Her flowing robes, unlike those of the simple white and blue adornment of the acolytes, were decorated with silver and gold designs. Pride was not forbidden in Desmiel's doctrines, and the Matron Superior took a few moments to savor the feeling.

The bells beckoned.

She chanced one last look at herself in the mirror, then turned toward her bedside table. Upon the table lay a slender knife. She took the weapon and slipped it into the sleeve of her robes. One could never be too careful, not when the portents of virgins spoke of danger.

Exiting her chambers, Clarissa was immediately beset by Elaynne, abbess of the convent. She was a slight woman, almost sickly in her stature and pale skin, but a cruel slyness flashed in her icy eyes. She was only a year younger than Clarissa. Indeed, they had served as acolytes together. At one time, they had been the closest of friends, confessing their darkest secrets and desires to each other. But that was decades past, and ambition and jealousies had torn their camaraderie asunder. Elaynne made no bones about it: she felt she, not Clarissa, deserved the mantle of Matron Superior.

"Sister Elaynne, if I didn't know better, I'd say you were concerned for my well-being. Every time I open my door, I find you lurking outside like a worried hen."

"Matron Superior." Elaynne stepped from the shadows, moving close. No other would be so bold as to approach Clarissa so intimately. "I'd have a word."

Clarissa paid the woman's incursion little mind as she turned from her door and strode down the hallway. Elaynne, undeterred, followed closely. The hem of her robes *swished* along the stone floor.

"I bring disturbing news," Elaynne said,

"Go on."

They continued on their way. The hall was gloomy and cold, for fire was a luxury only allowed in the warming chambers, the Matron Superior's personal chambers, and the infirmary. Pale moonlight and creeping fog filtered through the open windows lining the dreary corridors. The Order of the Sacred Visitation had learned to tolerate the cold and see in the shadows quite well.

"Some of the soldiers," Elaynne said, "they speak of an approaching darkness."

"Soldiers *always* speak of such things, Sister Elaynne. The horrors they inflict upon one another are never enough. They must look to demons and monsters to get their blood pumping. Coddle them as you would an infant." Clarissa looked back at her rival and arched an eyebrow. "It wouldn't be the first soldier who had sucked at your teat."

The Abbess drew in a sharp breath at the insult, and her eyes narrowed.

The bell rang out in the night.

"Is there something more?" Clarissa increased her pace. "It would seem the battlefield's bounty is never-ending. Or did you not hear the bells from your hiding spot outside my room?"

"I heard the bells quite clearly," Elaynne said. "The infirmary is already over-crowded, and I fear the smoke from the charnel fires will black out the moon before the night is through. But I thought this was important enough for your attention."

"And you thought wrong," Clarissa said, and she smiled to herself.

"The storm the soldiers speak of," the Abbess said, "is the Razing."

The word staggered Clarissa as surely as if she had been kicked in the stomach. She stopped and turned toward the Abbess. Elaynne, reading the surprise on the Matron's face, couldn't help but smile a little herself.

"The Razing?" Clarissa said. "It is a myth. Nothing more. What would you have me do?"

The Abbess watched Clarissa for several seconds before speaking.

"Close the gates," Elaynne said, "and let no one else enter the convent."

Even though Clarissa's voice remained low and calm, the Abbess shrank away from her.

"Have you forgotten our sacred duties so quickly? We do not turn away the sick and injured, no matter the rumors circulating in the infirmary…or the dormitories. I assume the Sisterhood has already heard this talk of the Razing."

Just as I am certain you helped to spread the gossip.

"Matron Superior," said Elaynne, "it is still within your power and your right to close the gates for a time…at least until we can be sure there is no threat. As you know, Sister Anna has predicted disaster befalling the convent."

"I'm startled at how quickly the gossip has spread." Clarissa's lips curled in a sardonic smile. "It was only a couple of hours ago that Anna spoke to me of her visions. It would almost seem as though someone waited outside my chamber to question the child when she left."

"The girl came to me," the Abbess said, "disturbed by your obvious lack of concern."

"I find that highly doubtful," Clarissa said. "Your charge may be to care for the Sisterhood, but you've never been one in whom they would be eager to confide."

"Be that as it may, my words of caution remain unchanged."

"I'm not sure what game you're playing," Clarissa

said, "but allow me to offer some cautioning words of my own. Perhaps you'd be less concerned if you spent more time at prayer and less time with your plotting. This is the last I'll hear of turning our charges away... unless you would like to spend the next few days in the misericord."

Elaynne took a step back and lowered her head.

Clarissa was well-pleased at the ease at which she had cowed her adversary.

The bells tolled.

The flood was only just beginning.

SEVEN

Foolish cow!

Sister Elaynne strode along the corridor, and the cold night mist did little to cool her temper. She chewed at her lower lip, biting so hard she drew blood. Her eyes burned, but she refused to let herself cry. She was no simpering little girl, and the Matron Superior didn't deserve the victory. She was more angry at herself than anything. She had expected Clarissa's reaction. She had even expected the sharp nature of the woman's words. But no matter how many times she had been berated by the woman, she still felt vulnerable and small and at least a little frightened in her presence, and for that she was furious.

She'll damn us all with her pride!

The Matron was insane. There could be no other explanation. The pressures of her position had been too much to bear, and she had finally snapped. Why else would she keep the gates open when the threat of the Razing loomed so closely? Why else would she ignore the dreams that haunted the girl, Anna? Adherence to the strictures of their faith was all well and good, but not at the peril of the order itself.

The bitch so fears betrayal that she'll betray every woman in the order!

The Matron Superior so jealously guarded her title

and position that she saw skullduggery at every turn. Her paranoia insulated her from everyone around her. Her pride blinded her to sound counsel. And now she might doom every man and woman within the convent.

Good.

She needed the Matron Superior to be paranoid… to be proud. It was suspicion and self-importance that would be the woman's downfall, and Elaynne was next in line to assume the mantel of leadership.

Assuming she didn't die first.

A group of nuns hurried down the hall toward her. They wore the attire of full-fledged sisters, not aco-lytes, and they carried themselves with the nagging demeanor of frantic hens—a disposition too many of the flock seemed to develop with age. Elaynne would have gladly traded the lot of them for the mewling, wet-behind-the-ears naivety of the acolytes. As Abbess, though, it was her duty to see to the needs and concerns of the Sisterhood.

"Abbess…there is a stranger at the gates."

"Another soldier seeking care," Elaynne guessed. "Let him in. Despite our warnings, the Matron refuses to seal the gates."

The hens grew more anxious. They chattered and cried, seeming to speak as a singular, many-headed thing instead of a group of rational women. One would start a sentence, and the next would finish, as if they shared the same harried mind.

"But…the rumors…"

"…is the Matron Superior unconcerned…"

"…rumors of grim tidings…"

"…the flesh-eater…"

Just as the Matron Superior was a victim of her own paranoia, pride, and madness, it would seem the Abbess was victim to her own orchestrations. As Clarissa so clearly suspected, Elaynne had made doubly sure the rumors of the Razing—and of Anna's cataclysmic visions—had spread through the Sisterhood. In this way she had sown the seeds of doubt in the Matron's capabilities. It was all going according to plan—perhaps too well. She was already dealing with the fallout, and the ceaseless prattling of the nuns gave her a headache.

From the middle of the cacophonous chatter, one of the sisters spoke up.

"Abbess," she said, "I don't believe the stranger is a warrior at all."

Sister Prin was not so easily swayed to worry as the others. She took fair measure of her surroundings and the events unfolding around her before she carefully chose how she would react. She was smart. Worse, she was without a doubt a supporter of the Matron Superior.

The other nuns fell into a hushed whisper as Elaynne regarded Prin.

"You have some insight to impart, sister?"

"The newcomer is a woman," said Sister Prin.

"A woman?"

"Yes…and she carries the seal of a healer."

EIGHT

The newcomer was a woman, after all, lithe and pale, dressed in leather wrappings and a heavy cloak as black as her long hair. Her hair concealed her eyes, but she raised her head to look toward the sisters who watched from the convent walls. She held a healer's bag in one hand. Around her neck was a healer's emblem, blooming vines writhing through the eyes of a skull.

Elaynne, standing among a clutch of confused and worried nuns, eyed the woman.

Neither Elaynne nor the newcomer said a word.

"She is not dressed as a healer," said Sister Prin.

"Could she serve another order?" asked another sister.

"We are thousands of miles from any other healer's order," said Elaynne, "More likely, she stole the symbol. Or found it. Or forged it herself. Such a thing is not unheard of. A healer's mark is quite valuable in times of war, allowing one to move through battle-ravaged lands untouched and unharmed."

The woman looked up at them. She did not call out for entry. She did not beg. It was as if she simply understood that she would be allowed into the convent, as if it was a foregone conclusion.

The woman's certainty troubled Elaynne, troubled her and angered her.

A *lesson*, Elaynne thought. *A lesson in humility would serve her well. When she approaches our gates, when she looks upon those who can grant or refuse entry, she should do so with a measure of respect. Perhaps I have no control of the Matron Superior's actions, but here—at this moment—the power over this woman's fate lies in my hand and in my hand alone! Let's see if her bold demeanor breaks when I cast her back into—*

The woman smiled.

The change in her expression was slight. If anyone other than Elaynne noticed, they said nothing. The corners of the newcomer's lips rose—not much, but enough. Her eyes, partially concealed beneath the veil of dark hair, narrowed. It was as if she knew some secret, a secret she expected to be revealed to the Sisterhood at any moment.

A man's gruff cry rose from the darkness. "Open the gates! We have injured men here! Let us in!"

Torchlight flickered from the darkness, accompanied by the shuffling crunch of booted feet. Shadows pulled away from the emptiness, and a contingent of warriors moved toward the gates. There were a dozen men, hunched over and weak, their tunics and cloaks ripped and stained with blood—their own, as well as the blood of the men they had surely left dying on the field of war.

"Open up!" The leader of the group—a man who

clutched at his stomach to keep his guts from spilling out—bellowed with what little breath he had left. "Save my men! You took an oath!"

With that, the man staggered to a stop and pitched forward. He stood just behind the woman in black. For a second, it appeared as if he would fall against her. His size and the weight of his ruined armor would have surely brought her down. The woman, though, sensed the man's collapse. Without looking back at him, she stepped to the side, letting him sprawl to the stone. She never took her eyes off Elaynne. Her cold smile never left her face.

The dead man's blood spread across the stone.

The wounded soldiers shuffled past, stepping over the body of the man who had spoken on their behalf.

Elaynne cursed under her breath.

"Let them in," she hissed. "Let them all in."

And the massive gates creaked open.

NINE

I'll be damned, Kast thought, *if I'll let these devils bring me down.*

Leaping over a downed tree, almost slipping in the mud, he moved through the forest. He was quick, yes, but not graceful. Men of Kast's size, men carrying such muscle, seldom moved with elegance. Instead, his every step was one of efficiency and purpose. He was driven. Those who saw him striding through the forest might have believed that he had shorn the fallen tree in half with his great, black-bladed sword. They might believe that another tree would collapse before him if it dared to cross his path.

Kast was tall and strong, clothed in tall boots, a leather kilt, sturdy bracers, and a heavy cloak. His long, dark hair was damp with sweat. The scars of countless battles covered his face, chest, arms, and legs. Hardly an inch of his rugged flesh was unmarked by scars.

The echoes of grim deeds.

He heard footsteps behind him, the rustle of figures moving through trees, the rattle of armor. Gruff voices grumbled at one another, giving direction.

"He went this way!"

"We're close now!"

"Ready those arrows!"

They would overtake him at any moment.

It was all part of the plan.

Kast hated the plan.

Ducking behind a tree, Kast planted his back against the trunk and held his sword at the ready.

The men burst through the forest. Six of them. Lean and vicious and hungry, garbed in the colors of Lord Rajenva's forces. Three carried swords. Another carried an ax, the blade of which was clumped with gore from previous battles. Two others held arrows nocked in their bows. They were anxious and eager to run their prey to ground.

Kast could not see them, not from his hiding spot behind the tree. He did not need to. He could hear their movement—lacking both grace and efficiency. Their ragged breathing and panting. The creak of bowstrings held back and at the ready. He could smell the oil upon the swords. Their sweat. The blood and rot on the axeblade.

His muscles tensed.

Soggy brush squished underfoot as the warriors drew closer.

Kast's grip tightened upon the hilt of his sword.

The axman moved past the tree, never once glancing in Kast's direction.

Until it was too late.

With both hands, Kast swung the sword. The black blade caught the axman in the stomach, crushing organs and spine alike, nearly tearing its victim in half, lifting him off the ground, and hurling him—unwanted—away. The axman's sundered corpse smashed into one of the archers, sending him sprawling into the mud and dead leaves.

Kast emerged from behind the tree, his muscles rippling, his sword dripping blood. He stepped on the gore-caked ax which his first victim had dropped, and defied the others to come forward.

The archer—the one who was not struggling to pick himself up from beneath the entrail-spilling body of his cohort—took aim and fired. The arrow sank deep into the trunk of the tree, inches from Kast's head. Kast looked at the arrow, marveling at the lack of accuracy. Did Rajenva no longer train his troops? Was the man simply unseasoned by battle? Or was he simply too lazy to try when it came to death-dealing? Kast rolled his eyes toward the archer.

"All right," he growled. "You're next."

And the archer's head went flying.

Kast waded into the remaining soldiers, shredding them with malicious, cleaving blows. One swordsman went flying, spattering blood in a pinwheel pattern. Another lost both his hand and his head. The third collapsed to the ground, gurgling for mercy, after his own blade was shattered and fragments of steel pierced both of his eyes. Kast offered him none. With a chopping sweep, Kast nearly cut an the mewling warrior in twain. He grabbed the final man—the archer—by the throat.

"I'll never hear the end of this," Kast muttered.

The archer, unable to breathe, wheezed and kicked

feebly at the forest floor. Tears ran down his cheeks as he gazed back at Kast.

"The plan," Kast said, "was to let you wound me so I might be taken to the healers."

Bubbles of spittle popped in the archer's trembling lips.

"But I didn't like that plan," Kast said. "Why should I allow worms like yourself to slice away at me? Better than you have tried, and they've been rewarded with a grave for their effort."

The archer's eyes rolled back in his head.

"Plans change," Kast said. "I'll get into the convent, my friend, but not because of any wound you might inflict."

The archer went limp in the grip of Kast's massive hand. Without air, he had passed out. Kast regarded the man for a few seconds. He was young, maybe no more than 18 summers. If he had been raised in Kast's tribe, he would have already seen countless battles. But this boy grew up in the comfort of the High Kingdoms. Chances are, this was the first war he had seen. If he survived the coming days of battle, he might have a full life ahead of him.

With a twist, Kast snapped the archer's neck.

"Plans change."

He let the body crumple to the ground. As the man fell, his quiver spilled it contents. The arrows—the fletching black and red, the color of Xendraken's banners—clattered and rolled across the forest floor. Kast picked up one of the arrows, musing at how many red and black birds had to offer up their feathers so a vain lord's archers could mark their shots. He twirled the arrow with his fingers.

His fist clenched the shaft, and he slammed the arrowhead down, embedding it deep in the meat of his thigh.

He clenched his teeth at the searing pain.

Pulling his hand away from the arrow, he watched the blood pool around the puckering wound, gathering around the shaft before oozing down his leg.

Not bad, Kast thought, *but it will not convince a nun that I am in dire need.*

"Another, then," he spat, and reached for a second arrow.

TEN

"You look proud," Matron Clarissa said, examining the newcomer through narrowed eyes.

"Proud?" asked the woman. Her voice expressed little more emotion than her near-blank expression. She cocked her head slightly, a bird-like movement, almost as if she did not recognize the word.

Clarissa allowed herself to smile, just slightly, letting the darkly clad woman know that a Matron Superior of the Holy Order of Sacred Visitation was not one to be trifled with.

"Smug," Clarissa said. "It's unbecoming."

"Why would I be smug?" the newcomer asked. "Rather, I'm thankful that you would welcome me into your home."

"You are not welcomed. Our gates were opened for the wounded. Only those who need our care lest they perish...only they and those who have committed themselves to the Sisterhood...are ever allowed to enter these halls."

"And yet..."

"Here you are."

The woman stared back at Clarissa. Her eyes were very dark, and though she was young, there was no sign of innocencein her gaze. She tilted her head in the other direction. Now, Clarissa noticed the slightest of scars on the newcomer's face. Not just one scar. Many. Dozens of barely-visible, crisscrossing scars, each one betraying a razor's edge cut that had healed long ago.

"What is your name?" Clarissa asked.

"Siris."

The name came out as a warning hiss, the first hint of emotion from the speaker, though her expression did not change.

"You carry a healer's seal," Clarissa said. "I've seen forgeries, to be sure. Such an emblem affords travelers safe passage, even among the most blood-thirsty of warriors. But the bag of surgical tools you carry—that tells me you know something of our art."

"I apprenticed with the Physician's Guild, cut my teeth during the Slum Riots of Orgroth. I earned my mark."

"The Slum Riots. Those were dark times. Danger-ous times."

"I remember."

"And yet you are not pledged to a hospitaller's order."

"I have found that in these times of strife, I can be of more worth by wandering. There are many battles—endless battles—being fought throughout the lands. Some are not so close to a sanctuary such as this one."

"A field healer."

"I help those I can, bring peace to those I cannot."

Silence swelled between the two women as

Clarissa took measure of Siris. In some ways, this young woman reminded her of Anna. They were both gifted—Anna with her visions and Siris in some strange way that could not be identified just yet. Anna, though, was pure and innocent and untested. Siris, on the other hand, was haunted. She had experienced darkness. She had been broken. And she had been built back up.

Siris inspired curiosity.

"You can stay," Clarissa said at last. "You'll be expected to aid us as we tend to our patients. And you'll follow our every rule. Do you understand?"

"Of course," said Siris.

Clarissa wasn't sure she believed her guest.

But it did not matter.

Siris had been broken before.

If need be, she could be broken again.

ELEVEN

Stepping from the chamber and closing the door behind her, Siris cursed herself with a smile, letting the tiny scars stretch on her pale skin. Most people didn't notice the scars, not until they were too close and it was too late. But the Matron Superior had spotted them straight away.

Siris liked the woman. She liked her sharp eye. Her cunning words. Her derisive threats. She liked her petty jealousies. She liked the murderous intent she saw in her eyes.

She knew she wanted me dead within seconds of meeting me, Siris thought. *Just as quickly as she spotted my scars. No doubt she's already made plans as to how she might kill me.*

She shuddered with anticipation.

She might want to torture me too.

She liked her.

Liked the uncertainty she brought to the game.

An unexpected turn of events, to be sure, but not one that changed anything.

After all, I knew how I'd kill her as soon as I saw her too.

But Siris wasn't here to have fun. There was a plan to be tended. There would be time enough for bloodied hands and laughter once the scheme had been carried out.

"Has she charmed you?"

Siris tensed and whirled toward the voice. Hidden in her robes, her hand found the handle of one of her many sharp, needle-like blades.

"I'm sorry, child. I did not mean to startle you."

A woman stepped from the shadows. She was the same age as the Matron Superior, though she wore her years a little more openly, clothed in the garments of a nun. Her eyes were kind, almost playful, and she smiled with a sweetness that almost sugarcoated a cunning, devious nature. Her hands were clutched together. She moved silently.

"The Matron Superior often has that effect," the nun said. "She's disarming. I suppose that's how you'd describe it."

Siris relaxed her grip on her blade.

"I am Sister Elaynne," the nun said. "I'm the Abbess—"

"I recognize you," Siris said. "When I stood outside the gates, it was you who looked down at me, you who considered whether or not to let me enter."

"That is one of my duties, yes, taking the measure of those who seek entry during these troubled times."

Siris bowed her head.

"Thank you, Sister Elaynne. Thank you for letting me in. I owe you a great debt."

Siris allowed herself another smile, a devious one, knowing the veil of her hair concealed the expression. The tiny scars on her face pulled taut once more.

Elaynne cleared her throat.

"What is your name, child?"

"I am Siris."

"Yes, yes. A healer from far away, is it? We're glad to have you. We'll put your skills to good use. Come with me. I'll help you get settled in."

Elaynne turned away and started down the hall. For a moment, Siris stood at the closed door to the Matron Superior's chamber. Elaynne glanced back over her shoulder, raised an eyebrow, and continued on her way. Siris hurried to catch up.

"I was not charmed by her," Siris said.

"Well, then," Elaynne said, "you're a good deal smarter than most of the other women you'll find scurrying about these halls."

"Have you not succumbed to her allure?"

"Me? No, child. I've been here a long time. I've seen her like come and go."

"If you have been here as long as you say—"

"Why am I not Matron Superior?" Elaynne finished the question. "I considered it. But, as I said, they come and go. When they leave, when their charms abandon them, it is rarely pretty."

And you, Siris thought, *long to see the Matron Superior fall.*

With the approach of darkness, the stone floors, walls, and ceiling turned black as obsidian. The convent was quiet here, every motion a whisper threatening to shatter the peace. Siris knew, though, that elsewhere in the fortress, the screams of the dying rang out in the shadow.

"The Matron Superior," Siris said, "keeps her quarters far from those you've sworn to aid."

"I suppose she does," said Elaynne.

"But not that far."

Siris tilted her head and held her breath. Silence filled the hall, yes, far from the beds of dying men. Still, she heard them, distantly at first, faint, but agonized screaming just the same. The sound swelled in Siris's ears, rushing across the stones toward her, drawn to her, buffeting her like a physical thing. She held her hands out at her sides, welcoming it, letting the shrieks wash over her.

"I can hear them."

Hearing nothing, Elaynne regarded Siris curiously.

"You're a strange one," Elaynne said.

Siris let her gaze trail across the hall. The sound was so clear to her, she would not have been surprised if it took visible shape.

"Come along," Elaynne said. "We must get you something more appropriate to wear. A hospitaller's gown. Looking the way you do, you're more likely to be thought a specter—a handmaiden of death—than a healer."

"We can't have that," Siris said.

Bells rang in the darkness, a sudden cacophony of disparate clanging. This time, Elaynne heard the sound. She did not stop walking. She did not so much as pause. In fact, she quickened her pace as she glanced at Siris.

"Your new gown will have to wait," she said.

"That's all right," said Siris. "This one suits me just fine."

"The bells mean we have new patients to tend. I'm afraid they ring more often than not these days."

"Will the Matron Superior join us as well?"

"Don't worry over her, child. She has more important concerns. It will be her choosing if she walks these halls tonight. But—yes, yes—she'll know we're at our work. She'll hear the bells."

She'll hear the screams before this is done.

She followed the Abbess down the corridor.

You all will.

TWELVE

"You don't look like one of ours."

The soldier eyed Kast as they shuffled toward the convent that loomed in the distance, jutting out of the jagged mountainside like a gigantic blade erupting from stone-like flesh. Kast had joined the company of injured men on their pilgrimage to the convent. He had simply staggered, bleeding, out of the woods to walk alongside them. No one had so much as batted an eye.

Until now.

"I'm speaking to you," the soldier said.

He was a head shorter than Kast, older, with deep wrinkles around his eyes, snot and flecks of blood in his beard. He might have been a captain of the guard. He might have been a common yeoman. His rank mattered little now. He was missing his right hand, and he used his left to clutch at the bloody stump. He had staunched the flow of blood by wrapping his cloak around it, but the cloth was soaked with a red so deep it was almost black. Kast could smell the infection in the man's flesh from three feet away. He would be dead in hours. Not even the healers in the convent would be able to save him.

"What's wrong?" he asked. "Are you deaf?"

"I hear you," Kast said.

"You don't look like one of Lord Grevely's men. You have no beard. You don't wear our colors."

"I wear the colors of your enemy." Kast eyed the red and black fletching of the arrows that jutted from his body. "Let's call it even."

"A sell-sword, perhaps?" the one-handed man said. "With no allegiance, save to coin. Ether that... or a filthy deserter."

The soldier spoke the word "deserter" more loudly, drawing the attention of the other injured warriors. Some of them squinted coldly toward Kast. Some of them turned to face him. Some of them touched the hilts of their swords or the hafts of their axes.

"I bear wounds, the same as you." Kast's hand fell to his black sword's hilt as well. "I bleed the same as you. I seek healing, the same as you. Look there—the convent rises before us. It would be a shame if you tried to turn me away now. It would be a shame if some of us didn't reach our destination now that we're so close."

The soldiers stepped back, wisely deciding that Kast was more interested in a scuffle than they were.

The one-handed man chewed at the inside of his cheek. Sweat beaded on his forehead and on his lip. At last, he spat.

"Feh! Who gives a shit if you are a deserter and a coward? You're here now!"

He shuffled ahead, feigning sudden disinterest in Kast.

Up ahead, a bell tolled.

"Come along, men," the one-handed man said. "The holy women are calling."

The soldiers turned away from Kast and moved on.

The path to the convent was littered with dead men, soldiers who had succumbed to their wounds and fallen to the wayside. Kast's companions muttered curt prayers for those who wore the colors of their lord and master. They spat upon those who wore their enemy's colors. Kast offered neither prayer nor spit. He could spare neither at the moment. But he noted that the bodies had been stripped of armor, weapons, and—he assumed—coin purses alike.

"Picked clean," the one-handed man muttered. "Razing take whoever did this. If I find them, I'll gut them on the spot."

Doubtful, Kast thought.

Emerging from the forested path, Kast looked upon the towered fortress of the Convent of the Sacred Visitation. Ravens hunched on the high ramparts, glowering at the visitors. More corpses—robbed of their valuables—lay upon the rocky ground leading up to a vast stone bridge. The bridge, decorated with footprints of old blood, spanned a deep chasm. More bodies, Kast imagined, littered the craggy bottom of the chasm, and he wondered if they, too, had been looted.

The bell tolled.

The heavy wooden gates began to rise.

The one-handed man staggered, losing his footing, almost falling. Kast grabbed him by the arm and kept him upright. The dying soldier looked at Kast, surprise on his ashen, sweaty face. The fever was upon him.

"Come on," Kast said. "You'll die, but at least you'll do so in a bed."

From a landing above the gates, a cluster of healing women watched. They were clothed in whites and pale blues. All save one, who wore shadow blacks. Her dark hair shrouded her pale, emotionless face and her cold eyes.

Death, waiting among the angels.

Kast's eyes met hers, but only for a moment.

The Sisterhood welcomed them.

And Siris was among them.

THIRTEEEN

With a damp rag, Siris wiped sweat from the forehead of a dying man. She sat on the edge of the bed beside him, regarding his pale face, his bloodshot and pain-filled eyes, his nostrils flaring, trying to breathe in as much air with his last breaths as possible. She dipped the rag into a bowl of cool water, rang it out in her fist, and wiped his trembling lips, his neck.

"You're not a nun," he rasped.

"A specter, I've been told." Siris plunged the rag into the water once more.

"Have you come to take me? Are you here to spirit me away?"

"If I am—" Siris glanced around a chamber filled with more beds than she could quickly count. Each bed filled witha bleeding or broken or burned man. And more patients still, sprawled on the floor between cots or sitting with their backs against the walls. "—it looks like I'll have a busy night."

"Aye." The dying man coughed out a laugh. "I had a bag of coins. Not much, but hard-earned. It's gone now, along with my sword, my armor, and my boots. The sisters work quickly."

"So I've heard."

"But I spotted you first. Jerrin Sol. That's my name.

Mark it on your black scroll. I claim the top spot on your list."

"Are you so ready to die, Jerrin Sol?" Siris asked.

If you are, she thought, *I can certainly speed you on your way.*

"Doesn't matter if I'm ready, does it? The darkness is coming for me, as black as those robes of yours."

"Yes."

"Best not to wait."

He turned his head to look toward the window. In the distance, the mountainous remnants of the Anderhalls rose like jagged shadows against the night sky. The Dancing Stars were bright tonight, three bright pinpoints moving in a slow circle around a fourth, brighter light. A rare sight, especially this time of year, and thought to be a good omen for both birth and death.

"It'll swallow up those stars," Jerrin said.

"What will?"

"Don't pretend you don't know. It's you that birthed it into the world. You set it loose on us."

Siris set the rag and bowl aside and reached into her healer's bag.

"What lesson were you hoping to teach us?" Jerrin asked. "Were you trying to tell us to stop all the fighting?"

"I'm not who you think I am."

Her fingers closed around a long needle in her bag.

"You are." He clutched at her forearm. "And I don't

want to see it. I don't want to be here when the Razing comes to take what's left."

"The Razing."

"I know we should have shown you more respect."

"You have naught to apologize for."

Siris slid the needle in under his arm. The point entered through a pore in his skin, spreading it wide. Polished steel sank deep, sliding in with ease, through muscle and tissue, straight into his heart.

Jerrin released her arm and fell still on the bed.

"Another one for the charnel fire?"

The question came from over Siris's shoulder, far too close for her liking. Sliding the needle out as smoothly as she had slid it in, Siris rose, turning, concealing the implement behind her back.

"Another one?" the girl asked again.

She was slight and beautiful. Her face was fresh, though a speckling of blood decorated her cheek. Under her arm, she held a basket overfull with bloody bandages bound for the wash.

"I'm afraid so," Siris said.

He thought I was Death made flesh, and I didn't want to disappoint him.

"You only arrived recently," the girl said.

"Just in time to ply my trade."

"I think I dreamed you."

"Dreamed?"

"I saw your arrival in a vision, I believe, and you were not alone."

"Of course not," Siris said. "I arrived with a host

of injured men. The war draws ever closer, the battlefield expanding. It's a wonder the gates are ever closed."

"There has been talk of sealing the gates." The girl leaned in close, dropped her voice to a whisper. "I've heard Sister Elaynne suggest such a thing. She fears what follows the dead."

"Do you?"

"I've seen it, too. I've seen the Razing. I've seen the doom that it brings."

Her heartbeat quickening, Siris looked once more to the nearby window.

It will swallow up the stars.

"In my dream..." the girl said.

Yes, yes. Speak of your prophecies. I'll show you something you didn't see coming.

"...you didn't come to help."

"No?"

"You came to steal."

Siris considered stabbing the girl with the needle. She knew a spot that would draw only a little blood but would create a deadly bubble of air traveling through her veins. The girl would be dead within seconds.

"To steal?" Siris asked. "From dying men? Do I look like a grave robber?"

"Sometimes, I dream of the future," the girl said, "but sometimes a dream is just a dream."

"Sometimes, yes." Siris stepped in close and drew in a deep breath. "You must be careful with dreams, for they cannot be trusted, especially those brought on by Gorgon Root."

"I...I don't..."

"Of course, you do. I can smell it on you. It lingers on your breath. It comes out in your sweat. A sweet smell, but treacherous."

"Let me help you." The girl set her basket aside and hurried to the bed. "We should clear the bed. Others need it."

The young sister had seen something in Siris's dark eyes. She wanted to change the subject. She wanted to distract Siris.

Maybe she can see the future after all.

Secretly, Siris returned her needle to her healer's bag. She worked with the girl to move Jerrin's body. Siris gathered up the sheets at the man's feet. The girl gathered them around his head, shrouding his face. They lifted him from the bed and lay him, wrapped in the blankets, upon the stone floor. Almost as soon as the corpse had been removed, another pair of nuns set about replacing the bedding.

"Someone will come for the body." The young nun gathered up her basket. "Our time is best spent with the living."

"And cleaning bloody rags," Siris said.

The girl stepped back, almost as if slapped. Her lips moved feebly as her mind chased an answer. She turned and hurried away.

No doubt she'll have another dream about me tonight.

A damning dream. And she'll tell someone who believes in her gifts.

"Making friends, I see."

Kast lay in a bed nearby, propping himself on an elbow and smirking at Siris.

Some of the other sisters looked in his direction, as if his bemused words had rang loudly and clearly among the moans and whimpers of the other patients.

"She is my sister," Siris told him.

"Seems so," Kast said. "Seems she knew quite a bit about you."

Siris shot Kast a warning look, then rushed out of the chamber to find where a young nun might rinse blood from cloth.

FOURTEEN

"What is it, then?" Deklir asked. "Some sort of sickness?"

Hod paid the younger man no attention. His knees popped loudly as he crouched next to a corpse. A leather necklace peeked out from under the collar of the dead man's jerkin. Hod tugged at the necklace to reveal a small copper medallion—the symbol of Threkus the Fierce, whose blessing would make a warrior unstoppable in battle.

"Must not have been watching out for you today, hey?"

Hod sneered and pulled at the necklace until it tore free. He pocketed the medallion. Gods above and below willing, he wouldn't need any aid in battle, but the bauble might fetch him a few coins.

Moonlight bathed the clearing in pale light. Blood— spattered across the ground and upon nearby tree trunks—looked black as pitch in the eerie glow.

Deklir searched another fallen soldier a few yards away. Using a small knife, he cut a small pouch from the man's belt. Without checking the contents, he pocketed the pouch and looked over his shoulder, as if to make sure he was not being watched.

Distantly, carried on the wind through the tangled trees, the sounds of battle could be heard. The cries of men—in anger or in agony. The metallic clatter of blade against blade.

"Hod—"

"Don't worry about that," Hod growled. "There's always a skirmish going on somewhere nearby these days. But that fight's not as close as it sounds."

Hod moved to the next corpse. These poor bastards had been cut to pieces, he thought, hacked down by the kind of brutal monster who took the fun right out of a war. He chuckled and set about looting.

"So, what is it?" Deklir asked. "The Razing—is it some sort of disease?"

"It follows the dead," Hod muttered, "same as us."

"What does that mean?"

"It means you'd best not dwell on it. It's not a sickness, boy. Leave it at that and get back to work."

They had been lucky, finding these dead men out here in the woods. Hod and Deklir had been following the war for some time now, and they'd collected a good many valuables. They had been on their way to the next vulture-haunted battlefield when they stumbled on this grim scene. A surprise, to be sure, but worth the few minutes it might take for a quick search.

"Hod the Ghoul," they called him back home, but he didn't care. The dead didn't need money. And old Hod wouldn't starve when the months turned lean, as they relentlessly did every year. Besides, he wasn't the only one who robbed corpses. He had heard many stories about—

"What happened here?" Deklir asked.

"You're full of questions today, aren't you?" Hod tugged the boots off a dead man, turned them over to see if a few coins had been hidden inside.

"Just curious, is all. There's six dead men here, all of them wearing Rajenva's colors. I don't see any of Grevely's men about."

"Ambush, most likely."

"They lost, right?"

"They lost everything, by Uthral's blood, and we pick the bones clean. Hurry it up now. We should be on our way. We're not the only scavengers following the war."

The wind shifted.

It carried the rancid smell of rot.

And the sound of flapping wings.

"Do you hear that?" Deklir asked. "What is it?"

"I don't think either us of wants to know." Hod abandoned the dead man he was searching. "Let's make haste."

But Deklir looked to the sky. His mouth fell open in horrific awe. He staggered back a half-step, another, and then stood frozen.

A wave of chaotic darkness spread across the moon.

An undulating black ribbon of winged madness.

A flock of nightmares swarming through the night sky.

"That's it," Deklir whispered at last.

"The Razing," Hod muttered. "By the gods—the Razing!"

The swarm swooped down, a spiraling cloud of flapping insanity, through the trees.

They came for the dead.

But they took the living just the same.

FIFTEEN

The bed smelled of old sweat and even older filth, a stink that had settled deep into the fibers of the mattress, roused by the slightest movement. More than a dozen similar beds, all stinking, all filled with wounded soldiers who would add their own smell to the air, filled the room. The stone floor was stained brown in spots from blood that was not mopped away quickly enough. Braziers of hot coals heated the space—keeping it too warm for Kast's liking—were positioned in a row down the center of the room. Open windows allowed sunlight and the occasional breeze to enter the chamber. Nuns moved from bed to bed, tending bandages, offering water, wiping sweat from brows.

What were they called? Which saint did they serve? The ever-presence of war must have kept the hospital filled, but the warriors who filled the beds most likely didn't understand much about the women who treated them. Likewise, the nuns themselves most likely knew little of the bleeding and broken men or the causes for which they fought.

It mattered little, Kast supposed. He did not pray to saints or to gods or to demons. He did not serve any warlord's cause. But he had few other concerns to keep himself occupied.

Kast turned his attention to the other warriors in the room, but their groans and whimpers and weakened sighs only served to irritate him. Here was a man with his face nearly caved in from the crushing blow of a Morningstar. There was a boy—barely in his teens—who had lost his eyes to a sword stroke. There was a gibbering man who sat up in bed, trying to count the minutes or hours or days on fingers that he no longer possessed. Most of those who survived their stay in the convent, Kast thought, would not be fit for the battlefield. They'd stagger out into the world without purpose. Few of them would even be able to lift their—

Looking to his bedside, Kast took note of his gear—his clothing and belt and boots and bracers, yes, but most certainly his black-bladed sword—neatly arranged nearby.

Some of the other patients possessed no weapons or armor. Perhaps they no longer needed them. But he doubted they had been brought into these halls without armaments or protection.

Missing from his own belongings, he noticed, was his leather pouch of coins.

"Vultures!" Across the way, a man who had lost both his legs writhed in his bed and cried out in misery. "They're vultures is what they are! These bitches! They bring us here so they can pick our bones clean! They take our weapons! They take our money!"

A couple of nuns hurried to his side, offering him water from a bowl.

"I don't want your poison!" he spat. "You've already taken my legs! You've taken my money! Now you want to take my life!"

The picture of patience, the sisters spoke softly to the man and guided the bowl to his lips. After a few more complaints, he drank, but he eyed the women with mistrust and anger and...

Helplessness.

"How are you feeling?"

A young sister with a round face and dark eyes approached Kast's bedside. She carried a pitcher of water, a bowl, and several yellowed but clean rags. She set the pitcher on the table next to the bed and crouched next to him to examine his dressings.

"Your wounds are clean," she said. "You should count yourself lucky. So many of the men we care for are sickened by infection, their own bodies, their own blood turning against them."

Kast said nothing. He did not tell her that he had treated his own wounds with herbs and plant extracts that had been used by his people to treat inflammation and disease for centuries. He had been taught to make a healing compress before he was five winters old. A blade in the night might kill him, but not a fever.

"You're mending quite nicely," the young woman said. "You'll only be with us for a few more days."

"I suspect you're right."

"If some beds don't become available soon, we might need you to offer yours up. It depends on when more wounded are brought to us. We'll make you as comfortable as possible, of course, but you're one of our stronger patients. And the strong must aid the weak."

"Let me guess," Kast muttered. "That phrase is carved into the stone above a doorway somewhere in this convent."

The round-faced girl watched him, a slight smile on her lips.

"It is one of our guiding lights," she said.

"Good for you." Kast glanced around the chamber, eyeing the pitiful, trembling, twitching patients, the men-at-arms laid low by cold steel. "And don't worry. There will be beds opening up soon, I'd imagine."

"Some of these men...they are your friends."

"I have...a friend among you."

Kast smirked grimly at his own words. Siris would hate that he was playing games. He was bored, though, and the young nun amused him.

"Here." The girl grabbed the pitcher and poured water into the bowl. "Drink this."

The water looked clean and cool, and Kast's throat was dry. He hesitated, though, and eyed the legless man across the way. He lay still, his eyes open, his mouth agape. A pair of nuns set about wrapping him in his sheets. Kast rolled his gaze to the round-faced sister.

"It looks like another bed is opening up," he said.

"Drink." The nun offered him the bowl.

"Is it poison?"

And now she smirked a little. Maybe she was bored, too. Maybe Kast amused her.

"It's only water."

Kast believed her.

But he did not drink.

SIXTEEN

The swarm swept through the forest, past gnarled trees whose roots had feasted on blood, across windswept crags adorned with shattered skulls and sundered bones, over rivers with water running red.

Flapping wildly, moving like a cloud of smoke, the swarm descended upon a battlefield where dozens of dead men lay sprawled in pools of gore and wreathes of their own entrails. Their only company, the flies and the crows and those warriors who had not yet breathed their last.

Dying men gazed into the darkening sky and shuddered in dread. Black as night. Bat-like, yes, but not bats at all. The frantic creatures had no bodies to speak of, no heads, no eyes. They had only their leathery wings and a snapping, sharp-toothed maw. Surely, this was Hell, come to claim the fallen warriors for their sins. With their final breaths, the men screamed.

"The Razing! It's the Razing! It's come for us!"

The swarm did not know its own name.

The swarm did not understand the force that had awakened it.

The swarm only knew the hunger.

Never touching the ground, the Razing scoured the battlefield, picking flesh—living and dead alike—from bones, then tearing the bones themselves apart. They took the flies, too. And even though the carrion birds scattered to the sky to make their escape, the Razing flapped after them, overtaking them and devouring them right out of the air.

Not even the blood was left.

It was as if the Razing had suckled every stone and blade of grass and grain of soil.

Weapons and armor were left behind, yes, and the metal gleamed with the Razing's passing.

No blood adorned the blades or the torn and twisted metal of the armor.

Still starving, the swarm whirled and spun into the air once more, seeing its next meal.

And there was death on the air.

The Razing smelled it.

They writhed in a sheet.

The swarm did not know that the fortress it approached was a place of healing.

The swarm only knew the hunger.

That was enough.

SEVENTEEN

In darkness, the legless man stirred.

His head spun, thoughts darting this way and that through his mind like frightened fish, and he could barely catch onto one before it wriggled free and slipped away.

Bitches!

…and…

Pick our bones clean!

…and…

Vultures!

…and most clearly of all…

Where am I?

He lay on his belly, damp and cold stone beneath him. Blindly, he reached out with trembling fingers, clawing at the floor, finding nothing.

They drugged me! Drugged me and threw me into the dungeon!

Thankfully, whatever they had given him dulled the pain of his lost legs, but he was dimly aware that the medicines were wearing off, and as his senses grew sharper, so would his agony.

Threw me down here to starve and waste away!

His fingers found purchase on the stone, and he pulled himself along. He couldn't be sure where he was going or what he would find, but at least he was moving. He had fought for years in the service of Lord Grevely, and he had learned that sometimes the difference between living and rotting was nothing more than a willingness to keep moving while suffering.

Keep—

—moving?

Something moved in the darkness.

Something besides the legless man.

It crawled in the shadows. The legless man heard its nails scrabbling against stone. It moved around him, circling him.

Too big to be a rat.

"Get away from me!" he spat, and he swiped his hand thr-ough the air, trying to scare off the unseen creature that stalked him.

A dog, maybe?

Had the nuns tossed him in the kennel? The air stank plenty, a rank and unclean stench. He heard no growls or snarls or barking, but the thing in the darkness moved around cautiously, sniffing him out like a feral hound.

The legless man pulled himself along the floor, faster now, desperate to discover a path to safety.

The dog—if it was a dog—prowled alongside him, keeping pace.

Now, he heard the creature taking ragged, eager breaths.

It smelled his blood.

It wanted it.

It drew closer.

Bitches! he thought. *Fed me to their hounds!*

And the beast fell upon him, forcing him down to the cold floor. Its stinking breath was hot on his skin. Its claws tore at the meat of his body. Its fangs ripped at his throat.

They did not feel like the teeth of a dog.

EIGHTTEEN

Fingertips trailed along stone walls.

The walls had stories to tell, stories of pain and suffering and treachery, but they were silent. The telling of such tales, Siris knew, might topple kingdoms. A lonely convent in the mountains would never survive such revelations.

Walls value nothing more than their own survival.

Siris had wandered far from the healer's ward. She no longer heard the screams of the patients. She found that she missed the agonized shrieking, the whispered words of kindness and hope—so untrue—from the nuns, the ragged death rattles of those who died believing the promises of the sisters. But she had work to which to attend. There would be time for idle pleasantries later. Not here. Other places in the world would be filled with lies and belief and shrieking.

Down a winding flight and along a silent corridor, she crept. Though she had never set foot in the convent before this visit, she felt that she knew the way. She had imagined it time and time again over the past several weeks.

The stories of an aged mercenary had brought her to this place. She had tended him months ago in the

Cathedrals of Navier, a place not so unlike the Convent of Sacred Visitation. He had spoken so vividly of the convent, even with Siris's hands buried up to the wrists in his stomach.

"Treasure," he had murmured. "They collect it from those they tend. Every man who seeks their healing pays a tithe, whether he knows it or not, and some pay more than others."

He had taken a spear to the gut, and most of his innards had been torn out along with the jagged point of the weapon. Siris did not expect him to survive, but it was so rare to find a still living specimen to examine and practice upon, let alone hold a conversation with. Now, as he spoke of hidden wealth, she found herself compelled to keep him breathing for reasons other than the academic.

"Have you seen many hospitals?" Siris had asked the old warrior, trying to keep him engaged and alert, even as his intestines slipped through her lithe fingers.

"Indeed," he had replied, his voice a whisper. "I'm old, but that doesn't mean I'm a skilled warrior. I've spent more time in a sick bed than I have on the field of battle."

"But this convent," she asked, "had a store of wealth?"

"After the Feud of the Ancients, my comrades and I were taken there to heal. Two hundred of us went through those gates. Only a couple dozen came out.

And all of us who returned were far poorer than we were at the outset. Some of the men complained that their payment for the battle had been stolen by the nuns. I didn't believe them at first, but I should have."

The old warrior started to fade, his eyes fluttering, and Siris squeezed and yanked at his entrails to snap him back to the here and now.

"Where do they keep this treasure?"

"The lower levels. I was out of bed, sneaking through the halls, looking for wine, when I spied it. Saw three of the sisters wheeling a cart of armor and blades and gold-filled sacks to a secret chamber. They threw it down to the depths. And that's not all. Men—men I fought beside and who were on the mend—were tossed through that doorway, too. And I stayed hidden, because I didn't want to join them, but I heard them screaming from down below."

"I would love to see such a sight."

"Lass," the old man had breathed, "I'll draw you a damned map...if you see to it that I walk out of this room alive."

In the end, he had not drawn a map, but he offered Siris detailed guidance to the hidden treasure trove. For her part and to her surprise, Siris had nursed the man back from the brink of death. The wounds he had suffered in his most recent battle did not kill him.

So, she smothered him with a pillow.

She could not, after all, have him telling anyone and everyone about the secret wealth of the Sisterhood.

A number of doors lined the passage, but Siris was unconcerned with all but one.

"The fifth doorway after the stairs," the old myrmidon had said.

The door was locked, of course. Siris had expected nothing else. She could pick the lock, she believed, given enough time. And she was meant to fetch Kast from the infirmary as soon as she discovered the door. He could bash the door in with ease.

She detected a coldness radiating from the other side of the door.

Coldness and the smell of death.

How many injured men had been cast into the basement to rot?

She would find out soon enough. She could count the moldering corpses while she traipsed among the fortune of countless ages. She found that she didn't want to wait. She felt a thrill at the idea of seeing the horde first. Kast would forgive her impatience, she knew. The pair had made a career of forgiving each other's transgressions, and this would be a minor affront amid other cruelties and betrayals and deceptions.

It was the capacity to forgive that made friends of the murderous and mad.

Siris reached into her healer's bag, digging for implements made to cut and sew flesh. They would dig at the mechanism of the lock as easily as they stitched the inner workings of the human body.

She was so thrilled by the secrets the locked door held, she failed to notice that she was no longer alone.

"You should not be here," Sister Elaynne said.

NINETEEN

Through a haze of lotus-mist, Clarissa watched the girl.

Anna spasmed in her seat, her wrists and ankles bound to the chair, a block of wood between her teeth and strapped to her head. For those gifted with fore-sight, use of the dream lotus came with risks. Under the influence of the mists, seers had been known to claw out their own eyes, to throw themselves from windows, to bite off their own tongues rather than share the secrets they had learned. Anna whimpered and mewled. He fingers flexed open and closed. Her eyes rolled wildly in her skull.

Three bowls of incense burned around her. Smoke curled, heavy in the air, twisting like ghosts. The smell was acrid and sweet, like funerary flowers, and tendrils of the mist reached for Anna's nose and ears and eyes and mouth. It seeped past the bite block. It brought tears to her eyes. It flowed into her nostrils with every panicked breath she took.

The Matron Superior breathed deep. The lotus-mist did not trouble her. It brought no visions, no risk of madness.

And she hated Anna for being special.

Several other sisters stood around the chamber, watching, bearing witness. Like their leader, they were not blessed with the sight. They were useful only in their devotion and obedience.

Clarissa moved to the girl's side and worked to free the wooden block from her mouth.

"What do you see, child?"

Anna drew in a sharp breath.

"Tell me what shall come to pass!" Clarissa demanded.

"Th-thieves!" Anna thrashed her head from side to side, as if fighting to speak the words. "Thieves are upon us!"

The Matron grabbed Anna's face by her cheeks, forcing her to hold still. She looked into her large, innocent eyes. Tears ran down the girl's cheeks.

"We have let them into our house," Anna said.

"Siris," the Matron urged, "she came here to steal from us."

"Y-Yes."

"She seeks the vault."

"She knows where to find it."

"She has help, doesn't she?"

Anna trembled, nodding, a puppet responding to the Matron's commands.

"She's worse than a thief, isn't she?" Clarissa asked, barely a question, pushing the child to reveal the secrets she wanted brought to light.

"She means you harm," Anna said. "She means to kill you."

Tenderly, the Matron caressed the girl's face. She straightened, turning away from Anna, and she looked at the other sisters, standing in the shadows and haze, their dark robes like shrouds.

"What must we do?" Clarissa asked.

As with Anna's visions, she already knew the answer she wanted.

"Punishment," the sisters answered in unison.

The Matron Superior smiled.

TWENTY

Sister Elaynne stood at the end of the hall, her hands clutched together, her face calm, as if she had expected to find Siris in this place all along.

"You followed me," Siris said.

"I did not," Elaynne said. "I've been waiting for you."

"What is this place?" Siris touched the door, felt cold seeping through the wood. "What will I find beyond this door?"

"You already know, don't you? It's why you're here."

Siris cocked her head. Her eyes narrowed. She hesitantly took her hand from the door.

"Who do you think I am?" she asked.

"A thief in the night, disguised as a healer, shrouded as a dark angel, but you're not here to treat the wounded. You've heard the rumors, haven't you? You've heard that we steal from the dead."

"Not just the dead."

Elaynne smiled sweetly. "No."

"You take the wealth of your patients, the few who live and the many who die. You secret it away in the bowels of the convent. How much, I wonder? How many treasures can be found below?"

"We have been here for many years," Elaynne said, "and there have been many wars in that time."

"What purpose does all that wealth serve?" Siris asked.

"Does it matter to the burglar?"

"I'm curious."

"Would it change your motivations if I told you we used our...earnings to treat the sick? If our wealth fed the hungry, would you leave our halls?"

"Not empty-handed."

"At one time," Elaynne sighed, "we used our money for the good of the convent and, in turn, for the good of those who needed our help: the weak, the frightened, the hungry, those who had been displaced by the ceaseless fighting. Over the years, though, our charity gave way to greed. The wealth serves no purpose, not anymore, and yet we continue to collect it."

"So, you won't miss it."

"I hold onto hope," Elaynne said, "that when the Matron Superior is gone, the money will be put to good use."

"If you wanted her gone," Siris said, "you would have done away with her long ago."

"I am not a murderer."

"You're not. If I decide to throw open this door—" Siris turned to Elaynne, stepping toward her. "—you would not be able to stop me."

"The catacombs are protected."

"I see no guards, none other than you."

"I might help you."

"Why?"

"You might kill me if I don't."

"I might kill you if you do."

Elaynne reached into her robes to retrieve a key. She held it tightly. She fidgeted with it.

"If I had been able to see the future," she said, "I could have prevented the Matron Superior from taking power. I could not have imagined how terrible she would be. How far she would take us from our mission. I never realized what she would become. Now, she is too strong. I am too weak."

"Is this a confession?" Siris asked.

"If I help you, perhaps you'll help me."

And now Siris detected desperation in Sister Elaynne's voice. She was not worried about the wealth below. She was worried about the order itself. She had sat idly by while the Matron Superior rose to power, and now the Sisterhood suffered for it. She was, though, a weak and frightened woman, able to plot and plan, skilled at small acts of aggression, but unable or unwilling to take a final, decisive action.

"Help me," Elaynne said, "and you can leave this place as a savior rather than a thief."

There was something unspoken in Elaynne's request.

She did not want to speak the truth of what she wanted.

She did not want Siris to utter aloud her understanding of the exchange.

It did not matter.

Neither or them—Siris nor Elaynne—had noticed the other figures gliding, as quiet as shadows, down the staircase or the hall. They had not realized they were being watched. But as the leader among the shadows spoke, Elaynne's eyes grew large, and she jumped. Siris felt the slightest and most sardonic of grins pull at the scars around her lips.

"You plot treason," the Matron Superior said. "Treason and assassination."

Clarissa stood before them, her hands clasped together gently, eyes gleaming with sinister delight. She could barely suppress a smile. She was accompanied by five other nuns. Four of them were severe and cruel-looking creatures, matching expressions of cold disapproval forever etched on their faces. The fifth was Anna, the young sister Siris had met earlier. The girl kept her head down, her eyes focused on the cracks in the stone floor.

Elaynne stepped forward, a plea already forming on her trembling lips.

"Matron Superior—I found Siris lurking about our halls."

The truth, Siris thought.

"She was seeking access to the catacombs."

Another truth.

"I tried to stop her."

She uses honesty as a weapon.

The Matron eyed them coldly.

But it will not help.

With a glance, the Matron issued a silent command to her companions. The four cruel-faced women surged forward. They surrounded Elaynne, like carrion birds surrounding a piece of dead flesh, pushing her back several steps. Uselessly, Elaynne struggled to slip past them. Then, she looked to the Matron and shrieked for forgiveness.

"Please, Matron Superior! Please! I've always been loyal to you!"

And there's the lie.

"You are a traitor," the Matron said. "And you will pay the traitor's price."

The four nuns who surrounded Elaynne drew long, sharp daggers from their robes. They were crude weapons, not so elegant as the blades Siris used, but they were not forged for elegance. They were made for chopping, for tearing meat, for making a visible example of their victim.

Elaynne screamed.

The daggers rose and fell. Each time they fell, they came back up more bloody.

Elaynne threw her arms up for protection.

The daggers chopped at her, shredding through her skin.

Elaynne sank to the floor.

The daggers hacked through flesh, scraped against bone.

"Please!"

Elaynne died, sprawled on the floor, with a gurgling plea on her blood-flecked lips.

The murder-nuns turned toward Siris, crowding in close, blood-slathered knives clutched in blood-slathered hands. Siris let her gaze tick to each of them, only for a second. She recognized that the first of the nuns moved stiffly, as though an old ache slowed her movements, especially on her left side. The second, despite her fearsome sneer, trembled ever so slightly in fear. The third stepped in Elaynne's spreading blood; her footing would be precarious in the slick gore. The fourth eyed Siris in a detached and clinical manner, sizing her up the way Siris sized them up. The fourth was a skilled killer. The fourth reminded Siris of herself.

She would die first.

"I want her alive," the Matron said.

Siris looked toward her.

"I have questions," the Matron said. "Bring her."

The four nuns grabbed Siris, dragging her roughly along.

Siris smiled.

They left Elaynne where she lay, brutally stabbed and hacked and chopped, crumpled upon a glistening sheet of dark red.

TWENTY-ONE

Waiting, Kast decided, was for stronger—and much more bored—men.

There was a plan, yes, but such schemes seldom played out the way they were meant to. A little chaos always reared its many-faceted head to spoil predictions and strategies and ploys. Kast would have it no other way.

He would not, however, lay in a sickbed while confusion and pandemonium washed over him.

He glanced at the other warriors, lost in medicine-fueled slumber. At the sisters, moving from patient to patient, silent as spirits.

Ghosts, he mused, *waiting to harvest ghosts from flesh.*
And he lingered among them.

It's likely Siris has found the treasure vault already.

He tossed the blankets aside and rose from the bed, dressing quickly, grabbing his black sword.

"What are you doing?" One of the nuns approached. "You should be resting."

"Your remedies have me feeling like my old self again," Kast said. "The beds are needed for other souls, or so I heard. The strong must aid the weak, after all."

"You should be resting," the nun repeated.

"I don't think you want me here any longer than I

need to be." A growl—a warning—seeped into Kast's words. "I'll be on my way."

"No, no." The sister looked around the room, hoping to spy someone other than herself to contend with Kast's stubbornness. She wasn't so naïve as to risk her own involvement. "If you must leave, I'll find someone to show you out."

While she scanned the room for someone she could boss around, Kast quietly slipped into the hall.

Siris kept her secrets, yes, and getting a straight answer out of her could be challenging even when she felt like sharing. But he had gleaned enough information from her to have some inkling where the convent's spoils might be housed.

I'll find Siris there, I'd wager, counting flies on corpses rather than counting gold.

He cared for Siris in his own way, but madness and bloodlust were her most faithful handmaidens. No plan, not even one of her own devising, often survived her whims. During the long trek to the Anderhalls, he had often heard her mumbling in her sleep about bringing sorrow and death to the Sisterhood. A smile had always flitted unconsciously across her lips while she dreamed.

Kill the sisters if you must, Kast thought, *but let's not lose sight of why we've come.*

And despite his gift for bloodshed, Kast's own proclivities leaned less toward death and more toward anarchy. He wanted to get rich, surely, but only because mayhem benefited from affluence. He knew a dozen revolutionaries who would name him saint for a price, twice as many madmen who would worship him as a god. And their fervor could bring the highest of walls crashing down.

A young nun—the round-faced girl he had spoken with earlier—emerged from around a corner. She carried a basket of clean bedding. She nearly collided with Kast, almost dropping the bedding in the process. She gaped wide-eyed at the towering warrior before her.

Kast held a finger to his lips, instructing her to be quiet.

She watched—soundlessly—as he continued on his way.

The young sister would doubt her silence many times throughout the evening. She would consider telling someone that she had seen the warrior lurking in the halls. The decision would weigh heavily upon her until she decided that her loyalty to the Sisterhood meant more than any sympathy she felt for the man. She would not reveal what she knew, however.

She would be long dead before she got the chance.

TWENTY-TWO

After a time, she knew only screaming.

With leather bindings cutting deep into the flesh of her wrists and ankles, Siris had been strapped down on the coarse table. She was on her stomach. Her hair sweaty and plastered to her face. Her black dress had been pulled from her shoulders, revealing the pale skin of her back, also covered in the razor-thin scars of hundreds of old lacerations.

She was no stranger to torture.

Yet she still screamed.

This pleased the Matron Superior. She watched as the sisters lashed at the young woman's back with leather straps, as they placed white-hot coins upon her skin, as they drove needles deep into her muscles and under her blackening fingernails. They added new scars to the old. They salted the fresh wounds. They relished their work. They savored it.

Serpents of blood slithered down Siris's back and dripped to the floor.

Anna, standing to the side, looked away, horrified by what she had witnessed, by what she had brought about with her visions.

Matron Clarissa raised a hand, giving pause to the torturers as she slipped across the room, coming closer. Siris's screams faded to mewling grunts. The Matron gave her a moment to catch her breath.

"Why have you come?"

Her voice was calm yet commanding, an unspoken promise that if Siris answered, the pain would end, but if she did not it would be much, much worse.

"Why are you here?"

Spittle falling from her lips, Siris sneered. "You already know."

"I don't want you to suffer," the Matron lied. "Tell me what I want to know, and I will make the pain stop."

"Why would I want that?"

She was mad, the Matron realized, longing to be tortured.

"You were caught trying to enter our vaults. You came here to steal from us."

"Yes."

"You're no healer."

"But I am."

"The mark you carry...it's not yours."

"I earned my mark."

"And you used your status to worm your way into our sanctuary."

"It looked as though you could use the extra help, what with so many of your sisters spending time robbing the sickly rather than treating them."

The Matron hissed. "You are not alone. Who is helping you?"

"You already know. You killed her. Sister Elaynne."

"She's lying," Anna said timidly. "I saw another."

Siris laughed painfully. She glared at Anna from behind strings of wet and tangled hair.

"We'll find your accomplice," the Matron said. "We'll conjure another vision if we must."

"We all use whatever talents we can," Siris said, "to 'worm' our way into the graces of our patrons."

Weary of the interrogation, the Matron motioned to the nuns. They resumed their work, slicing and piercing and flaying the skin of their prisoner.

But Siris had already gone numb to their toil.

And so she screamed.

She screamed at the nothingness, at the absence of feeling.

She screamed for something—anything—to fill the void within her.

The scream was as a powerful wind, blowing open the doorways of her mind.

She saw.

A storm of darkness. Black wings, flapping wildly, spinning through the air. They were born of death, festering up from accursed maggots in accursed flesh, and now they chased their sire, ever nipping at the heels of oblivion, feasting on the corpses that had been left upon the field of battle, but always hungry, never satisfied, and if they could not find decaying flesh to devour then they would feast upon the living.

"Th-they're coming!"

Siris spoke in ragged gasps, not because of the torture, but because of the vision that assaulted her.

"A vision," the Matron said.

Anna flinched. "She's lying! She's not been given the medicine! She sees nothing!"

"I think she does," the Matron said.

"They'll be here soon!"

"Who?" The Matron Superior was at Siris' side. "Who do you see?"

"Death's servants! The Razing!"

"Where are they?" The Matron asked.

Siris could see them swarming before her, their hooked and serrated wings battering against her, leaving tears in her pale skin. She reached for them, beckoning to them, but they cascaded away from her, just out of reach.

"M-more!" Siris pleaded with her torturers, pleading with her. "Don't stop!"

The nun looked at the Matron Superior.

"You heard her," the Matron said.

The nuns set about their bloody work.

And Siris saw the truth.

TWENTY-THREE

The dead woman upon the floor served as a marker.

She wore the garb of a nun, but the white and blue cloth was soaked in blood. She lay in a pool of red, a look of horror on her face.

This, Kast thought, *must be the place.*

She had been hacked at with zeal. With glee. This was not Siris's work. Oh, she enjoyed herself when she delivered death, but she also reveled in the preciseness of her craft. There was joy in these wounds, but little care. Little skill. Whoever had killed this woman had enjoyed themselves, but they hadn't made the enjoyment last.

Kast squatted next to her. In her bloodied fingers, she clutched a set of keys. He pried them from her stiffened grasp. Standing again, he turned to the door directly behind him. The fifth door after the stairs. The dead nun's blood oiled the lock as he slid the key into the mechanism.

As the lock was undone, a scream rang out from somewhere deep in the convent. Kast listened. He knew the sound.

Siris.

She was in pain. Suffering at cruel hands. Shrieking in darkness.

He would leave her to it.

She would have it no other way. If their roles were reversed, she would allow him to be tortured.

Only he would not enjoy it nearly as much.

The door swung open to a flight of stairs descending into nothingness.

Elsewhere in the convent, Siris screamed as she met her fate.

Kast's task—his challenge—awaited below.

Stepping lightly, Kast descended the stone staircase. He held the lantern in his left hand. The shadows were defiant and stubborn. They were accustomed to total dominance here in the bowels of the convent. The guttering lantern's glow, on the other hand, was timid and hesitant. It pushed the darkness back, but Kast knew better than to trust the light's loyalty. It would flee the first chance it got.

In his right hand, he clutched the hilt of his sword. There was no uncertainty there. The weapon had served him well time and time again. It would continue to serve him, by light of day or dead of night, for years to come. The sword was part of him, just as his heart and lungs and stomach were his own flesh and blood. If the sword failed him, it would mean his death.

As he reached the bottom step, Kast saw what the Sisterhood had been hiding.

Their secrets stood revealed.

The lantern illuminated a vast chamber filled with treasure. Light sparkled across fine swords and ornate suits of armor, helms forged to look like the faces of lions or hawks or sea creatures, shields decorated with runic symbols. A sea of coins covered the floor, islands of gemstones among the glittering silver and gold.

The legends of wyrm-hordes Kast had heard as a boy were nothing compared to what the hospitallers had collected.

The rumors were true.

For decades, the Sisterhood had treated the injured and the dying from countless wars. For decades, warriors had passed from this world into the next in the halls of the convent. For decades, the wealth of the fallen warriors had been gathered in the catacombs.

The sisters had more than they would ever need. An endless supply of soldiers continued to show up at their doorstep, promising more riches with every infected stab wound, ever shattered ribcage, every pulverized spine. Siris and Kast had come to alleviate the burden of such wealth.

Kast slid the toe of his boot through the spilled coins, wondering to himself how many of the convent's patients had died of the injuries they'd sustained on the battlefield and how many had died thanks to the Sisterhood's care. It didn't matter, though it seemed an act of cowardice to murder someone in their sick bed. Certainly, cowardice and treachery had utility, but Kast found such characteristics to be tasteless.

He moved deeper into the treasure trove, taking note of items of value, pocketing a few baubles along the way. Setting his lantern on the floor, he crouched and picked up a rugged gold coin marked with the symbols of Hyrnn, a fiefdom that had been conquered and eradicated more than twenty years ago. The coin danced in his fingers, catching the light on its dull surface. A warrior with a crown of fire was emblazoned on both sides. Kast scoffed. He had met more than one old, red-haired berserker who claimed to be from that fallen realm. They were bold, but they couldn't back up their claims. He flung the coin into the darkness. He heard it clatter against other treasures, roll across stone, and spin to a stop.

Something slid through the shadows.

As if disturbed by the thrown coin.

Coins hissed in the gloom as they slid across each other.

Kast grabbed up the lantern and thrust it in the direction of the sound.

The unseen presence slithered away from the light. Kast's hand tightened on his sword's hilt. Someone was down here with him, crawling unseen through the horde, staying just outside the lantern's glow, circling him.

Kast stepped forward.

The unseen figure moved away, coins clinking together.

He moved to the right.

The figure—A prisoner? A guardian?—scurried, moving on all fours from the sound of it, to the left.

He heard breathing now.

Ragged and labored and anxious.

Hungry.

A horror leaped out of the shadows to Kast's left. Withered and filthy and pale, flesh starkly white, draped in rotting rags, long and wild grey hair hanging down in clumps and tangles. A woman, Kast realized, and old. So incredibly old. She moved fast, though, striking out of the darkness with a feral quickness, and her fingernails and toenails were long and filthy and sharp.

Kast raised his left arm to ward her away. Hissing, the hag scratched at his flesh, digging deep. The lantern fell from his grip, clattering to the ground. Kast brought the pommel of his sword down upon the woman's head as she clawed at him. She fell away, landing on all fours near the lantern, and she looked up at him with pitch black eyes. Viscous drool spilled from her lips—lips that were stained red with blood of former victims. She spat a curse and swiped at the lantern, sending it spinning away, its light pulsing in the darkness.

The glow of the lantern was distant now, but it was enough that Kast could make out the almost sheet white flesh of the old woman. She loped around him, circling him, and he moved to face her, keeping his sword between them. His arm burned where she had gouged at his flesh, and his skin hung in tatters from the wounds.

The hag slashed at him with her clawed hand. She was faster and stronger than she should have been.

If she managed to rake her nails into Kast's throat... if she plunged them into his eyes...if she found a bleeding vein...she could prove to be deadly.

I'll kill her quick. Put her out of her misery.

Kast swiped his black blade at the hag's head, but she slipped out of the way, ducked in low, and clawed at his leg, slicing through his britches and the meat of his thigh. She smiled, then, an unfamiliar expression to her, the muscles of her face twitching weirdly. Kast slammed his sword down, but she leaped away.

Some people enjoy their misery too much to let another take it from them so easily.

And he could respect that.

Kast kicked her in the face.

The old woman might have been fast and strong, but Kast struck her with force that rivaled that of a charging boar. She flew backward, head over heel, and landed several feet away.

She landed like a spider.

She scrabbled toward Kast, on her fingertips and toes, hissing. In the dark, he slashed at her with his blade, but she scurried aside, slipped past him, jumping at him, grabbing at him, scratching at him with her nails. Kast grabbed her by the hair and yanked her head back. The force of the act might have broken a man's neck, but the old woman was made of sterner stuff. Kast flung her across the room. She struck the floor, sending coins flying, and rolled once again to her hands and feet.

Kast readied himself. When she leaped at him again, she'd find herself impaled upon his sword.

Only, she did not leap.

The hag turned her head, looking over her shoulder. A faint light fell across her hideous features. She smiled again, and this time it was not an unnatural expression. It was a smile of pure joy. Drool dribbled from her lips. A tear rolled down her pale cheek.

The door at the top of the long flight of stairs stood open.

She had been trapped in this treasure chamber for ages, Kast realized, feeding in the dark on whatever hapless victim the Sisterhood decided to toss into the shadows.

Now—she saw freedom.

The hag forgot about Kast. She moved up the stairs, still crawling like an animal. She was hesitant at first. But she picked up speed with every step as she climbed toward the convent above.

Kast watched her go, then turned his attention to more pressing—and profitable—matters.

TWENTY-FOUR

Clarissa sensed the truth of the prophecy. As Siris had muttered the words, there was a change in the very air. The shadows deepened. It was as if, somehow, Siris had willed some form of doom to manifest.

The fates, it was said, sang mournful songs that shaped the events of the world.

The Matron Superior exited the torture chamber. Anna, begging to be heard, followed.

"She's lying," Anna said. "She does not speak for the fates."

The girl was afraid. Afraid that she would not have value if Clarissa found herself another seer. Perhaps she was right.

"She only wanted a reprieve from the pain." Anna stayed close, reaching out, pleading. "She wanted to distract you with her deceptions."

Clarissa whirled on the young sister.

"Does it sound like she wanted a reprieve?"

As if in answer, Siris cried out in agony from down the hall.

"The pain awakened her visions," Clarissa said. "And she asked for more."

And pain, Clarissa thought, *is far easier to come by than dream lotus.*

"She is an aberration," Anna said. "She came here

to steal from us. She came to do us harm. I've been faithful. My visions have been offered freely."

Clarissa touched Anna's chin. "And the Sisterhood is thankful."

The Matron Superior released the girl and hurried up a flight of stairs. Cold night air rushed down to meet her.

"But she is false!" Anna said, lifting her dress to race after the Matron. "She mislead you! She mislead us all!"

The Matron reached the upper walkway. She stood in the open air, looking out across the mountaintops.

"Did she?" Clarissa asked.

Anna gasped.

In the distance, writhing like a serpent against the backdrop of the moon, a ribbon of shadow heaved and swelled and rolled.

"Can you imagine?" The Matron almost laughed. "Sister Elaynne thought that sealing the gates might protect us."

"What is that?" Anna asked.

"Don't you know?" Clarissa stared in awe at the rise and fall of the shadow. It reminded her of the movement of birds in a spinning flock. "It is the damnation you predicted. It is the devastation Siris foretold. It is our undoing."

"The Razing," Anna breathed.

"I always thought it was an illness," Clarissa said. "A plague. But look. Whatever these creatures are, they are alive. It is a horde."

"What do we do?" Anna I asked.

"Go, child. Warn the others. We must take cover."

"Cover?" Anna asked. "But—where?"

"The Razing looms near. Even as we have stood here, it is drawn ever closer. Go. Prepare your sisters."

Anna, still unsure but eager to please, hurried away.

What do I care where you hide? Clarissa thought. *This is our ending, and it is long overdue. The order is finished. But I know where I'll wait out the storm. And when I emerge once more, I will be a wealthy woman.*

TWENTY-FIVE

"I think...she's dead."

Their faces were spattered with blood. A red mist hung lazily in the air. Upon the table, the pale, dark-haired woman lay still, and a crimson sheen glistened over nearly every inch of her body.

"She's not moving."

The nuns gathered around. They clutched at their needles and blades and hooks with trembling, unsure fingers. A look of uncertainty passed between them.

"She's not breathing."

The sisters understood the Matron Superior's quick anger and relentless cruelty. Indeed, they had been chosen time and again to mete it out. They were her tools of pain and misery, just as the implements they wielded were theirs. And if the tools did not serve the Matron Superior's will, if they had grown dull, they would be cast out and replaced.

"What do we do?"

One of the sisters hurried to a nearby table, cast the scissors she held aside, and grabbed a leather bag of pungent corpse-salts.

"This will wake her!"

The stench of the corpse-salts nearly gagged the sisters. They sprinkled some—not too much, for it was known to have a loathsome effect if not used sparingly—under their subject's nose. The woman did not react.

"She's beyond our reach!"

Just then, they heard the tolling of bells.

"More patients have arrived!"

Instinctively, the sisters set about putting their tools away, wiping them clean, and arranging them neatly alongside one another, before washing their own hands in bowls of cold water.

"The bells! Listen! Something is not right!"

They took a moment to listen. The bells rang, but not in the steady fashion intended to summon the Sisterhood to their sacred task. The tolling was frantic and uneven.

"A warning! Something's wrong! What do we do?"

The sisters held their breath as they listened.

They had turned their backs on the dead woman.

They did not see her slip a blood-slicked wrist out of the leather strap that bound her.

TWENTY-SIX

Through the winding halls of the convent, Kast followed the screams.

The sound carried a chill, and the torches along the walls guttered as if caught in a strong wind. Embers spun through the air, dancing frantically to the music of the shrieking, whipping through the hall and out the open windows, fading, becoming one with the night beyond.

Siris.

He knew she could handle herself. He knew she was no stranger to torment. He knew it would take more than a few nuns to tear her from this world.

But the screams.

They sounded...different.

They did not belong to Siris.

And there was a strangeness in the air, wasn't there? Something was amiss. Kast felt it, deep in his bones. He had felt it...smelled it in the night...when he had taken the spoils of his exploration outside. The miasma of death was in the air. And the convent's bells chimed at its approach.

He was not one for superstition. He did not trust in the existence of magic. He did not believe in the gods. His faith was reserved for his own sweat and blood and muscle, for the feel of steel in his hand. But the presence he felt, the rush of an oncoming storm, was as real as the point of a sword driving toward his heart. Whatever was coming was not myth or legend. It was alive. And it was hungry.

Ravenous in the unending and unyielding manner of death.

The Razing.

An old warriors' tale, whispered around campfires and funeral pyres alike, an infernal swarm, worked into a frenzy by slaughter, sweeping the fallen from the blood-soaked battlefield, taking them to meet the countless gods of death, and since the living were so eager to meet their myriad and pathetic endings, they, too, would be taken to face judgement.

Pig shit.

Not the Razing. That was real enough, Kast surmised. But it served not the gods.

There were no gods of the dead, save the dirt and the worms therein.

Siris believed in such celestial presences. She claimed to see them, though they strode blindly and invisibly through the mortal realm. She claimed to speak to them, though they used no human tongue. She did not, though, claim to be their faithful servant. So much as Kast refused to believe in the gods, Siris refused to believe in piety.

The screaming stopped.

Kast made his way down the hall. He met a few nuns, but they paid him no mind. The unsteady and distraught tolling of the bells summoned them, and they had no time to tarry with a wanderer. Some of them were weeping as they hurried past.

He no longer heard the screams. He could not be sure where Siris was being held. His keen senses, his memory, had brought him this far. Now, he only needed a little luck. He'd find his partner, dispatch those who tormented her, and—

At the end of the hall, a door opened.

Siris emerged.

She moved timidly. She was in pain as she adjusted her black robes. Her ashen skin was covered in smears of blood, some her own, some belonging to others. Her medical bag was open and overfull. She had acquired several new surgical instruments. Some of them glistened and dripped.

At her side, Kast helped to steady Siris. He looked past her, into the room from which she had emerged. The shadows were heavy beyond the door, but the chamber had been turned into an abattoir.

"What did you do?" Kast asked.

"They wanted to see the future. I showed it to them." Siris looked at Kast, the slightest hint of a smile on her lips. "They didn't like what they saw."

"They never do."

"I wove a prayer into their flesh. We are blessed, you and I. We are beloved of dark spirits."

"Even if we weren't, I'd wager we could bribe our way past any god or devil."

"The treasure?"

"I found it, right where it was supposed to be. The

hospitallers have been stockpiling weapons and armor, coins and jewels, for decades. I gathered what I could, more than enough. We'll be able to fund the war effort for a half-dozen upstart warlords."

"The beast will be fed."

"And there will still be plenty for the two of us."

"I'd like to see Jehalen," Siris said, "a city of flower gardens and fountains and vineyards and boundless peace."

"Why not?" Kast said. "We can afford it."

"I'd like to watch it burn."

They made their way up a flight of stairs. Cool night air raced down to greet them, as did the sounds of shrieking and incessant leathery flapping.

TWENTY-SEVEN

The Matron Superior watched as her sisters died.

A swarm of black-winged nightmares swept through the courtyards and the halls and the stairwells of the convent. They were flapping, stinking, screeching horrors without any real bodies to speak of. No heads. No legs. Just wings and mouths and fangs. They moved in undulating, frenzied unison, overwhelming their prey, surrounding them, shrouding them, cutting them to ribbons in a matter of seconds, leaving nothing behind.

And this did not satisfy their ravenous hunger.

All around, sisters in bloodied robed ran for their lives. Some bled from terrible cuts or bites. Some flailed about, tearing futilely at winged creatures that clung to their bodies, ripping and tearing. Some gaped in disbelieving horror from mangled faces that had been denuded of skin.

And some, weeping, just collapsed to the floor and waited to be taken.

Struggling to keep herself from screaming, Clarissa pushed past her panicked sisters. She raced down the hall, past the healing chambers, which were filled now with a cloud of the flapping beasts. The bedridden warriors had been treated with medicines to help them sleep. They did not wake as their flesh and bones were devoured.

A small mercy.

But Clarissa did not intend to die tonight. As a few stray bat-like beasts swooped and dove toward her, she swatted them away. She knocked one from the air and crushed it to a bloody, bubbling pulp underfoot. She hurried down rough-hewn stairs.

The Razing had come.

Death had lured it to them.

It would billow down every hall, through every window, and it would eat and eat and eat until there was nothing left.

But there was a safe place. A room without windows. A chamber deep in the bowels of the convent where the Razing might not be able to find her. In one hand she clutched a ring of keys. In the other, a knife. She had brought the weapon—a blade laced with a deadly venom—to contend with the thing that dwelled in the darkness below. It was well past time to put the pitiful, imprisoned creature out of her misery anyway. And once she had dispatched the hag, she would wait out the Razing in the darkness below.

Among all the wealth the sisters had collected.

She reached the lower hallway.

And stopped.

The door to the chambers below stood open.

But...who could have done such a thing? The would-be thief—Siris—had not breeched the passage.

The blood that had been spilled upon the stone floor—Sister Elaynne's blood—remained. It had yet not been washed away. It had been smeared. Footprints tracked through it.

A man's boot.

Leading toward the door. Leading back out once more.

The thief.

One of the patients.

Aiding Siris.

Rage blossomed in her chest. The Sisterhood had spent decades gathering their riches, and in all that time, no one had dared steal from them. If not for the chaos in the halls above, she would have ventured back the way she came. She would have found the culprit and driven her knife into his chest. She would have carved out his heart and forced Siris to eat it little by little.

She would—

Another set of prints upon the floor caught her eye.

A woman's bare foot.

Leading away from the chamber.

Clarissa's breath caught in her throat.

The beast had escaped from below.

Her fingers tightened on the handle of the slender knife she carried. Perhaps she would not need the weapon after all. The hag had slipped away. With any luck at all, the nightmare swarm above had already picked her old bones clean.

Clarissa hurried down the hall. Skirting around the thickening blood, she moved toward the door.

"Matron Superior!"

Voices called out behind her. She snapped her head around to see four young sisters hurrying toward her. They were pale and frightened, trembling and weeping. Two of them bore terrible cuts on their faces and hands. The other two were uninjured, but their robes were stained with blood, perhaps of their companions, perhaps of their patients, perhaps of some unfortunate soul left behind.

"Save us!" they cried.

The sisters rushed toward her, ignoring the blood, even as they slipped in it. They crowded around her. They grasped at her, pleading, clawing at her as if trying to rend salvation from her flesh.

"Save us! Save us, please!"

Clarissa pulled away from them. She tried to force her way past them. But the nuns pressed in, ever closer, clutching desperately at her.

"The Razing is here!" The sisters pleaded with her for safety. "It's come for us! It will be on top of us soon!"

The Matron slashed at the frightened sisters with her knife. If she could not force her way past them, then she would cut her way to freedom. Blood jumped as the wounds the Matron Superior delivered crisscrossed with the cuts the bladed wings of the swarm had left behind. Still the sisters grabbed and scratched at her. Clarissa plunged the blade forward blindly. Steel sank into the neck of a young nun. Her eyes went wide. She clutched at her throat. She staggered back, falling, wrenching the slick knife from Clarissa's fingers and taking the weapon with her.

The other three barely noticed. They pressed in closer.

"Let me through!" Clarissa cried.

The sisters did not listen.

The keys were torn from Clarissa's grasp. She was struck, kicked. She fell, gasping, to the floor.

The three sisters left her there as they rushed to the open doorway. They threw the door open and pushed through into the darkness.

Clarissa staggered to her feet. She followed them, stepping over the body of the woman she had slain, desperately reaching out.

"Wait!" She cried.

As she reached to door, though, it was pushed closed. One of the sisters, her face marred by a terrible, bleeding wound, peered out at her, without pity, as she sealed the passage.

The Matron Superior nearly collapsed against the door. She clawed at it as if she might dig through the wood. She wept and mewled and begged for entrance.

Through the veil of tears, she saw a figure at the end of the hall.

A hideous, twisted, pale figure, dressed in tattered rags.

Her fingernails were long and sharp, caked with dirt and blood.

Her lips and chin were stained a blackish red.

Her eyes were wild.

The Matron pushed herself away from the door. She stood tall and defiant as she faced the old woman.

The hag's face split open in a terrible, rotten-tooth snarl.

With a howl, she surged down the hall, leaping like a feral thing.

The Matron Superior's resolve—her defiance—broke.

She ran for her life.

TWENTY-EIGHT

A cloud of razor-winged beasts churned above their heads, flapping wildly, screeching, so chaotically thick that they blocked out the moon and the stars.

Siris and Kast hurried along the high, open-air walkway. Kast didn't bother looking overhead. Nothing he might see in the frantic, flapping blackness would change his course. Siris, on the other hand, gazed up at the swarm with wide-eyed excitement and fascination.

"They're just as I envisioned!" she cried.

The path was littered with the ravaged corpses of the Sisterhood, their robes sodden with gore, blood pooling around them. Some had been picked almost to the bone, but small, bat-like horrors even now swooped over the bodies, nipping at them, tearing strips of flesh away.

A wail cut through the night, and a nun burst from a nearby corridor. A dozen or more winged horrors flew around her, diving, biting at her. She waved her hands, swatting at them, as she ran for the parapet. She threw herself over the side and plummeted, striking the jagged mountain walls, to the depths below.

"They're not attacking us," Siris gasped.

"They haven't noticed us yet," Kast said.

"There's more to it than that. I saw them. I saw them in my mind's eye. I think...I summoned them."

Kast glanced at Siris, his scowl proclaiming that not only did he disbelieve such nonsense, but he doubted Siris believed it, either.

Siris smiled sweetly.

As they passed under an archway, they saw a figure huddled in the shadows. It was Anna, the young sister, the girl with the visions. She was curled into a ball in a corner, sniveling and weeping, clutching at her knees with her hands. She whimpered and mewled.

Siris paused, approached the girl, and crouched next to her.

"Did you see them, too?" Siris asked.

"I—"

"Do not be afraid." Siris touched the girl's shoulder tenderly. "If you called to them, they will not harm you."

Kast growled. "Siris, we don't have time for this."

"Of course, we do." Siris shot a warning glance his way. "She beckoned to them, the same as me."

"I...don't know what you mean." Anna looked at her, confused but hopeful. "But, please, help me escape this place."

"The Razing will not harm you," Siris said. "Your visions protect you."

"My visions?" The girl shook her head. "No, no. I lied, don't you see? I saw some things, yes, but most of my prophecies were false. The lotus loosened my tongue and inspired deception. I offered up lies in hopes of ingratiating myself to the Matron Superior. I was...I was skilled at guesswork, perhaps. Sometimes the things I said came to pass. More often, I simply knew how to speak in vagaries that seemed to hold the promise of the future."

Siris cocked her head as she regarded the girl. To Kast it seemed that Siris was having difficulties comprehending what she was being told.

"You are a seer," Siris said.

"I'm not."

"You are, but you believed yourself false."

"Only sometimes," Anna answered. "And only because I wanted to make my life more comfortable."

"There is comfort," Siris said, "only in death."

She slid one of her long needles into Anna's throat. The young nun's eyes went wide. She twitched and spasmed and spilled to the stone floor. Siris regarded her curiously. Anna's eyes remained opened even as her blood jumped from her neck to spray a nearby wall.

What visions did death bring?

Kast took Siris by the arm. "We should go."

Everywhere they looked, the Razing wreaked havoc. Winged horrors sliced skin open and stripped flesh from bones and slurped up blood, screeching all the while.

A cluster of nuns ran past, among them the round-faced sister who had shown kindness to Kast. "Help us!" she screamed. Razor-winged horrors flapped around her. She was slashed in a dozen places. Blood seeped through her robes. A nasty cut ran down her forehead, across a ruined eye, splitting her nose and lips. She reached out desperately with twitching fingers. "Help us! Please!"

"A friend of yours?" Siris asked.

"She was kind," Kast muttered, indifferent.

"A pity."

One last encounter awaited the pair as they made there way through the convent.

This one made Siris giggle.

The Matron Superior lay on the stone floor. Her upturned face was a frozen mask of horror. Blood soaked her robes and spread in a pool around her. Her stomach had been ripped open. A hideous, twisted, feral old woman crouched over her, digging her long nails into the orifice, fishing up lengths of Matron's intestines. The hag dragged the entrails to her mouth and feasted greedily. Above, a cloud of black-winged horrors whirled wildly, but almost patiently, as if waiting for the withered old woman to finish a well-deserved meal before descending upon her for a feast of a different nature.

The Matron seemed to be looking at Siris.

The hag at Kast.

TWENTY-NINE

In the courtyard, four horses waited for them. Two of the beasts were burdened with bags that bulged with coins, overfull coffers tethered with rope, and small chests strapped down with leather. The other two were saddled and ready to ride. All of the animals were hitched to a post. They were afraid. The presence of the Razing unsettled them, and if the shadow-swarm swept into the immediate area it might have driven the horses to frothing madness.

Siris and Kast hurried to the horses.

Siris paused before climbing into the saddle. She cocked her head to the side, curious, and regarded Kast.

"Did you seek horses before you came looking for me?"

"It seemed reasonable at the time. We needed horses to carry our spoils."

"And how long did it take you to bring your loot up from below?"

"A trip or two."

"I see."

"I could have gone back for more."

"Yes."

"You had things under control, I thought."

"It's fine." Siris let her fingers play across the bags

of coin, then across trembling horseflesh. "It's good that you waited. My eyes have been opened. I have seen the truth of the Razing. I know what is coming for us."

"The truth?"

Siris grabbed her steed's mane and pulled herself into the saddle. "We have a long road ahead of us. And we'll not be funding warlords."

"Where are we going? What will we do with our loot?"

"We're going to build a church."

"A church?" Kast grumbled under his breath. "I'm no holy man."

"It will not be a place of holiness."

"A church is going to be expensive." Kast eyed the treasure he had stolen from the bowels of the convent. "Warmongers don't cost nearly so much as the penitent. I gathered what I could. There's plenty more yet that's been left behind. If we—"

"It will be enough."

Kast nodded and climbed into his saddle.

They rode.

Behind Siris and Kast, a storm of screams and blood and black wings swept through the convent.

Siris dreamed of the house of worship she would build.

"I've always wanted a horse of my own," Kast said.

But not so loudly that Siris would hear.

END BOOK ONE

THE BLOODLETTER'S PRAYER

BONUS SHORT STORY

The land, the Bloodletter remembered, was once fertile and rich, an expanse of lush fields and thick forests.

Now, though...

He crouched, running the fingers of his gloved hand over the dry, cracked earth. The movement stirred whispers of dust drifting across the ground. What was once abundant soil had shriveled to a barren, fractured shell where nothing could grow. One might think this place had never seen a drop of rain.

The Bloodletter rubbed his fingers together, letting the dust fall through the still air. He stood, looking into the distance, across the badlands. Desolation where there had been trees and crops, grass and streams of clear water.

And cities.

He had visited the great cities of old. He had studied within them when he was but an acolyte. He had studied in the spired libraries of Cereakis. He had been cut and beaten and trained in the art of the sword in the halls of Rellisar. He had been tortured in the scream-haunted dungeons of

Sendarken. Even now, decades later, he still bore the scars of his studies—across his back, his shoulders, his chest, his knuckles, and his face. An ache in his left wrist. A hitch in his right knee. His flesh, his muscles, his bones traced a history of grueling training and brutal ministries. The scars remained but Creakis, Rellisar, and Sendarken had all crumbled.

No rain, he mused, but blood in great supply. And blood did not yield crops or feed cities.

Ghosts, but no crops.

Once, before the gods went to war, he had been one of a thousand missionaries sent out with scriptures and blade to guide, to comfort, to protect, and to punish. Now, though, the mantle and robe of his order were threadbare and worn, his leathers scuffed and gouged. His chain of holy symbols and reliquaries had been cast into the dust years ago.

He no longer resembled a priest.

The blade at his side, though, still marked him as a Bloodletter.

He had wielded the sword while discharging his sacred duties. The blade was still sharp, honed in battle during his travels through the war-ravaged wastes, etched with the words of sacred texts. But while the sword served the same purpose as it had in the name of the gods above and below, it could not be described as the same weapon. Something had changed in the years after the Godwar. The Bloodletter had plunged the blade into the heart of the Mad Bishop, and the metal had been tainted by the slaying. Now, if one examined the signals closely, they might see the etched letters moving slowly, crawling around the blade, the words changing in blasphemous ways. If one listened closely, they might hear a chilling whisper, low and steady, as if the sword had forbidden secrets to share.

The Bloodletter had listened to these whispers and lamented.

These void-borne whispers had brought him to this wasteland, lured him with horrible promises.

The gods, the Whispering Blade vowed, have not abandoned the Cathedral of Vanris.

It spoke other promises, too.

But the Bloodletter knew it did not tell him everything.

The Bloodletter did not trust the sword. The Whispering Blade had saved his life more times than he could count, yes, but it also lied, hissed untruths with the same ease it spilled entrails and blood.

From a hiding place among standing stones, he watched the road to Vanris for hours. He grew more impatient—more certain that he wasted his time—with every passing minute. Soon, though, he saw a group of men marching along the path. They were monks, dressed in the dark robes of their order, heads shaved, skin tattooed with holy symbols. Chains marked with the symbols of a dozen gods—some of whom had loathed each other—were draped across their shoulders. Their feet were bare, kicking up little puffs of dust as they walked along. Swords hung at their sides.

A young boy—maybe eleven years of age—accompanied them. He wore the white robes of an acolyte who had not chosen his god. The monks surrounded him, protecting him as they continued on their pilgrimage.

The Bloodletter counted nine monks.

Nine men who would die.

They don't matter to their own gods, the Bloodletter thought. Why should they matter to me?

Only the boy was of consequence.

Sword in hand but held behind his back, the Bloodletter rose from his hiding spot and stepped out into the road. Holding his weapon as he did, he looked almost as if he was presenting himself formally and politely at the royal courts of old. These men might be approaching their own demise, but there was no need to be rude. The monks staggered to a stop when they saw him, and they drew their own swords, held them—uncivilly—at the ready. The boy's expression was blank. He did not acknowledge the Bloodletter.

"The boy," the Bloodletter said. "Leave him to me and you can go."

His voice, once so soothing and clear, was now a dry and quiet. It sounded strange to him. He had not spoken to anyone—not even himself—in many weeks. He sounded, he thought grimly, not unlike the whispering of his sword.

"Your heavens and your hells are overcrowded enough as it is," he continued, "and they are left untended. I can't imagine they are nice places to visit. So why be in a hurry to do so?"

Five of the monks stepped forward, their eyes narrowed, their lips curled in sneers.

"Heretic!" one of the monks hissed.

"Sin-spawn!" rasped another.

"Infidel!" cried another.

The Bloodletter had been called these names before, more often than not by men who would soon die upon his hissing, sigil-marked blade, men who would scream the names of vestigial gods as they fell screaming into the void, men who had served so devoutly in order to secure their place in the afterlife but who—upon death—find nothingness waiting for them.

Behind the Bloodletter's back, his hand tightened upon the hilt of his sword.

His muscles tensed.

He prepared to spring from his formal stance and into a death-dealing position.

With wickedly hooked and permanently blood-marked short swords, the monks came at the Bloodletter. The had wielded these blades in countless butcher-orgies to honor gods who represented lust as much as slaughter. They had sliced the throats of innocents in their beds to pay homage to the god of dreams and nightmares. They had disemboweled shackled unbelievers in the name of hungry, feeder gods. They were implements both holy and unholy, symbols of awful times when the great and terrible lords above and below had roamed freely.

Devotion and sacrifice bought each of the monks a half-dozen steps. As they charged, the Bloodletter welcomed them with vicious slashes and stabs, gutting them, opening their throats, piercing their chests. Their ceremonial blades fell to the dirt along with their spilled blood. Their faith did not save them.

The Bloodletter murdered without malice—murdered, even though he struck in defense of his own life, because he had come to kill these men. He had lain in wait for them. In his planning, he had killed each of them a dozen times already. His work was clean and efficient. In a matter of seconds, five men lay dead at his feet.

His sword whispered in delight.

Four monks remained. They had not thrown themselves at the Bloodletter as their retired had. This, the Bloodletter thought, showed them to be the most dangerous of their ilk. They would not fall so easily as the others. Three took up defensive positions before the fourth, who stood behind the boy. The fourth monk held the boy's arm tightly, yanking him back. He placed his hooked sword across the boy's neck and sneered.

"I'll kill him!" the fourth monk said. "Stand down or I'll open his throat! I know what you want, but you'll never have it! He'll not pray for you!"

The hissing blade urged the Bloodletter to strike.

The Bloodletter watched the monks. They were unafraid. They were bolstered by their faith, though it might be unrewarded. They were prepared to die for their beliefs, and they had been preparing to meet this destiny for years.

"Stand down!" the monk ordered once more.

The blade scratched at the boy's skin. A trickle of blood ran down his neck. He did not react in any way.

"You're bluffing." The Bloodletter took a step toward them. "If you kill him, you won't be able to use his gifts, either."

"Stay back!" the fourth monk commanded, panic in his voice.

The other monks clenched their weapons tightly. They braced themselves for the fight to come.

"There's no need for you to die," the Bloodletter said.

The hissing blade rasped in disagreement.

"Give the boy to me," the Bloodletter said, "and be on your way."

"Not another step!" The fourth monk cried. He shook the boy by the arm. He held his blade in a white-knuckled grasp. He was sweating and trembling.

He might just do it, the Bloodletter thought. He might slay the boy to prevent any prayer other than his own from being heard. He might actually be a believer.

A subtle shifting of his left foot through the dirt, and now the Bloodletter was in striking distance. Now he was poised to attack. He had already decided who would die first. The monk on the far right held his own blade in such a way that he'd be unable to parry an upward stroke coming in from the low left. The other two monks, scrambling in their surprise, would stumble into each other and be unprepared when the Bloodletter's sigil- and blood-covered blade changed direction and came for them in two inelegant but effective hacking strokes. With any luck, the Bloodletter would be done with them in such brutal speed that the fourth monk would be too stunned to carry out a murderous slash across the boy's throat.

But the monk on the left—the man who was the Bloodletter's intended third victim—cocked his head, taking notice of the hissing blade, and he gasped in fear.

"His sword! It's—"

The Bloodletter drove his blade through the man's throat before he could finish speaking.

Now, though, he had opened himself up to attack, and he could not pivot in time to avoid the slashing blades of the other monks. A hooked and blood-flecked sword bit into his right side. If it had not scraped against his ribs, it might have killed him. He growled in pain, drew his arm back sharply as he yanked the hissing blade from the dead man's throat. His elbow smashed one of the remaining monks in the nose, staggering him back, giving the Bloodletter some breathing room.

Ignoring the pain from the wound in his side, the Bloodletter whirled, and he claimed another life—and a pair of eyes—with a vicious, backhand slash.

The third monk drove his blade forward. Metal

screeched against metal as the Bloodletter parried the attack, knocking the monk's sword aside, then riposted stabbing his enemy through the heart.

Before the third man fell, the Bloodletter sprang at the fourth. The remaining monk wore an expression of fright and confusion. He was alone now, and his conviction to kill the boy faltered. Before he could regain his senses, the Bloodletter sank the hissing sword right through the man's mouth, silencing his useless invocations forever.

The hissing blade lapped up the blood.

To the Bloodletter, the whisper sounded a bit like, "gooooood boy!"

Panting and sweating, the Bloodletter stood among the child and dead men. He put a hand over the wound at his side. His clothing was sodden with blood, but he did not think the wound would do him in. It was more painful than deep. It could be tended later. He did not bother wiping the gore from his sword. He knew from experience that the blade would be clean within the hour, the blood seeping into the sword's slowly moving sigils. He looked toward the boy, who stood unafraid before him. He held his own pale hand to his throat where the monk's sword had scratched at him.

"Don't worry," the Bloodletter said. "You'll live."

"I... I'll live," the boy said.

"What is your name, boy?" asked the Bloodletter.

"Name?" the boy said.

The Bloodletter busied himself checking the bodies of

the monks. He did not like looting the dead, but even Bloodletters had to eat, and times had been lean since the Godwar had ended. He found only a few coins secreted away in the monks' robes. He found a small supply of Communion Dust, too, and he took that as well. He had no use for the hallucinogenic properties of the Dust, but some addicts he might encounter in his travels would pay a handsome price for it.

All the while, the boy stood nearby, waiting.

Waiting for guidance.

"Do you know where they were taking you?" the Bloodletter asked.

"Taking me?" the boy parroted.

"Never mind." The Bloodletter threw the last few baubles, coins, and a bit of food in his bag. He sat upon a stump and tended his bleeding cut, stitching it as best he could and placing a simple poultice of medicine—the last of his medicine—over the wound. Then, he motioned for the boy to join him. "Come on. We have a long road ahead of us."

Without argument, the boy followed.

The gods were not dead, though it wasn't for a lack of trying.

Long ago, they had flooded greedily into the world. They came by the hundreds, gods both great and small. They represented love or beauty, hate or murder. They boasted dominion over the sun, over the air, over the water, and over the earth itself. They were the gods of the harvest, of the hunt, of festivals. They were the lords of the wild places as well as the cities.

There were some that mused that every blade of grass had a deity associated with it.

Perhaps that had been true.

But all of the gods hated one another. They killed one another in order to claim spheres of influence the way some killers collect trophies from their victims. The god of cities became the god of cities and forests, though she knew not what to do with the latter. The god of the sun took the moon as his prize. The twin gods of disease became the gods of disease and feasts and of waterfowl.

Soon, their hate and rage and jealousy erupted into war.

The gods were all but wiped out. They died. They fled to hidden places. They vanished.

And they almost took the world with them.

Still, there were those who rejoiced at the thought that the gods yet lived. They uttered modest prayers. They scraped together meager offerings. They sacrificed livestock and let the carcasses rot while they themselves starved. One day, the monks and priests promised, the gods would return, and they would have learned humility, and they would rain miracles down upon the world that had suffered so at their hands. Mankind only need prove that they had not forgotten the gods.

"Bullshit," the Bloodletter spat.

He did not swear often. Such utterances had been forbidden by his order and now, when he was free to say whatever he pleased, there was rarely anyone to listen.

"B-Bullshit," the boy said.

The Bloodletter and the boy had traveled the rest of the day, not stopping until well after dark. The wound on the Bloodletter's side throbbed painfully with every step. His companion, however, had complained about nothing, and so the Bloodletter had kept his own grousing to himself.

Now, they sat by a small campfire, huddled close to the crackling flames as the cold crept in all around them. The boy stared into the flickering glow. The Bloodletter watched the boy for a while.

"What shall I call you?" The Bloodletter asked, talking more to himself than to the boy.

As much as the man was known for his profession—bloodletting—the boy was known for his lot in life. It was possible he had a name once. His parents might have named him when he was born, before they recognized him for what he was. His parents were likely long dead, and the name they had given the boy had died with him. He was a Prayer Vessel. His mind was empty, and his soul was pure. The purity might attract the attention of those gods who remembered the value of such things. The purity might also draw the baleful gaze of those who wanted to feed upon such a delicacy.

Either way, when the boy spoke, the gods above and below—forgotten though they may be—were likely to listen. The boy's emptiness meant that holy... or unholy... men might guide his words. They would speak their prayers to him, and he would parrot them to the gods, asking for blessings and miracles on behalf of someone else.

Maybe, the Bloodletter thought, that's why the gods listen to the Prayer Vessels, because they never want anything for themselves.

"I had a brother once," the Bloodletter said. "His name was Errol. He was an annoying little shit, always running his mouth when he should have been listening. That's what got him killed, I imagine. I always wanted him to be more like you. I wanted him to be quiet. I think I'll call you Errol, if it's all the same to you."

"Errol," the boy said.

Satisfied, the Bloodletter nodded, settled his back against the trunk of a tree and closed his eyes.

Some time later, the sound of singing woke him.

His hand went to the hilt of the Hissing Blade.

He jumped to his feet.

The Bloodletter knew many tales of ghosts and night-sirens and goblins that lured travelers with sweet songs. Such creatures were the messengers of the gods, and now that the gods had all but vanished, their emissaries grew confused and frightened and angry. They would fall upon hapless victims, torment and kill them, without cause and without mercy.

In that way, they were not unlike priests.

Or Bloodletters.

But there were no goblins, no apparitions or phantoms. Instead, Errol sat quietly, staring into the embers of the dying fire, singing softly and sweetly. The Bloodletter listened to the boy's soothing lullaby for several minutes. His fingers relaxed on the hilt of the Hissing Blade. The tension in his shoulders eased. The tune made the Bloodletter think about simpler, happier times, before he had been laden with the duty of slaying or cursed with the burden of the Hissing Sword.

He could not help but wonder, though, who the boy—the Prayer Vessel—was listening to as he sang.

Thus did even the thought of happier times fill the Bloodletter with unease.

Another two days of travel, and they reached the Temple of Vanris.

In the distance, a tall but crumbling temple rose from a barren wasteland of slate. The structure stood miles away, black against an angry red sky. A line of people—men and women, young and old, priests and penitents alike—stretched into the distance.

These hopeful worshippers shuffled forward — slowly, slowly — moving toward the temple step by step. Some carried valuables. Some brought chickens or kittens or small dogs in wooden cages. Others brought dried flowers or foodstuffs. A few bore hand-carved idols of warrior gods with multiple, sharp-toothed mouths. All carried prayers on their lips and in their hearts. All hoped the gods would hear their pleas.

Even as the Bloodletter and Errol approached the meandering line, more worshippers approached to join the procession. Still others could be seen in the distance. The line would continue on forever, especially considering that those who had already visited the far off temple would often march back to the end of the line, joining the group once again in hopes of getting their message to the god. At other temple sites, it was not unheard of for penitents to fall dead from exhaustion or malnourishment or exposure. When that happened, one of the people in line behind them would gather up the body as an offering to the deity that awaited them.

The Bloodletter did not join the procession. It moved too slowly for his tastes. He took Errol by the wrist and together they skirted along the line, passing the slow-moving penitents and the prayer-uttering holy men. The Bloodletter kept his eyes down, hoping that if he ignored the people in the line, they would in turn ignore him. It took maybe a dozen steps before this plan fell apart.

"You there!" A man called from the line. "Where do you think you're going?"

The Bloodletter paid him no mind. Clutching Errol's wrist tightly, he moved a little more quickly.

"Wait," another voice called. "Wait!"

Another yelled, "You can't just walk to the head of the line!"

"Stop, you!" cried another.

"Your prayers are no more important than mine!" said another.

Soon, the entirety of the line called out to him, a cacophonous riot of angry voices. Anger, the Bloodletter could contend with. He did not stop. But then he heard the exclamation he had been dreading.

"The boy! The boy's a Prayer Vessel!"

He quickened his pace, but it did little good. The temple was still quite a ways off. He and Errol would pass hundreds of desperate, pleading men and women. They no longer called for the Bloodletter and his companion to stop. Instead, they clutched at the boy, begging him to pass on their prayers.

"Tell him," an old man said, "that I served him well on the battlefields! Tell him I deserve my place in his Feast Hall!"

"Ask if my brother is by his side," said a red-eyed woman.

"My child," cried a desperate mother, "is so ill. I know he will not heal her, but perhaps he'll ask one of his brethren."

"I'm sorry for what I've done," whimpered another man. "You'll let him know I'm sorry, won't you?"

The Bloodletter moved along, dragging Errol step by step, ever closer to the massive temple. All along, the people standing in line grabbed at Errol, begging him to pass on their messages. The boy's lips moved as he spoke to himself, reciting to nothingness the hundreds of prayers that were passed on to him. The Bloodletter payed them as little mind as he was able. He did not want to hear their prayers. He did not want to know what they needed. He knew that the boy would not help them—far from it—and he didn't want to understand just how terribly they would be let down.

The worshippers nearly cheered as the Bloodletter and the Prayer Vessel reached the steps to the temple.

Fools, the Bloodletter thought. Poor fools.

He climbed the steps toward the enormous entrance to the temple. Once, the titanic metal doors had been sealed. Now, they stood open. The metal was dented as if the doors had been battered open by giant fists.

Within was a great hall, impossibly long, with a ceiling rising high above, held aloft by massive columns.

The real miracle, the Bloodletter thought, is that this place did not fall in the war.

He led Errol along the hall. The place was unlit, save for the light streaming in from beyond the great, battered doors. What awaited them at the far end of the temple was shrouded in darkness.

But it smelled of decay.

This was a tomb.

As the Bloodletter and the Prayer Vessel moved through the temple, a great silence rushed in around them. Even the boy, who had been echoing the desperate prayers he had heard outside, fell silent.

Before them rose the throne of a giant. The seat looked to have been carved from the floor itself, and it stood at least 30 feet high. Around the base of the throne were wilted flowers and moldy bread, rotted meat and gold coins, sacrificed livestock and pets, dried blood and even a severed finger or two—offerings to the thing that sat upon the throne.

The seated god was a skeletal horror, a withered behemoth that might once have been godly but was now horrendous. Withered flesh sloughed off thick bones and tusks. The thing slouched in the chair, its massive skull lolling to the side.

What god this was, the Bloodletter did not know, nor did he care.

He placed a hand on Errol's shoulder, guiding the boy to stand before him.

Errol gazed at the dead god.

"It's time," the Bloodletter said.

He drew the Whispering Blade.

"And I'm sorry."

The Bloodletter held his hissing sword next to the boy's ear. The runes crawled across the metal, the movement of the etched letters creaking, forming whispers.

The boy listened.

The boy spoke.

The Bloodletter squeezed his eyes shut. He tried to think of anything other than the words coming out of the boy's mouth. This was the Vile Tongue, a profane language of blasphemy and curses, of hatred and terror.

Tears rolled down Errol's face as he repeated what the sword told him.

He went on and on, and—listening, though he tried not to—the Bloodletter thought he might go mad. He wanted the boy to stop speaking. He wanted the sword to cease its ghastly whispering. He thought if it did not stop soon he might use the blade to hack the boy's head from his shoulders, though he wondered if even that might bring silence.

And then—just like that—the boy closed his mouth and lowered his head.

"Amen," Errol said.

All was quiet again, but only for a moment.

The dead god upon the throne drew a ragged and rattling breath. Its bones creaked as it shifted his enormous bulk. It slowly, painfully, gripped the arms of the chair and pushed itself to its feet. Dust fell from its body, hissing against the stone floor like rain.

The dead god did not acknowledge the Bloodletter or Errol as it stepped past. Its gait was unsure and unsteady as it lumbered toward the light at the end of the hall.

Errol moved to follow, but the Bloodletter held him back.

"You've done enough, boy. Neither one of us wants to see what comes next."

The dead god staggered through the open door to the temple. A great cry of wonder and adulation rose from the gathering of worshippers outside.

Soon enough, those cries turned to screams.

The Bloodletter watched Errol. The boy's eyes were wide with wonder as he listened to the shrieks coming from outside.

When he grew sick of the screams, the Bloodletter busied himself gathering coins from around the base of the throne. After all, the dead god had little interest in them.

Once the screaming stopped, the Bloodletter and the boy walked slowly to the door and exited the cathedral.

The dead god was gone, but he had left a trail of mutilated bodies in his wake. They had been torn apart, crushed underfoot, tossed around and broken. Every person in the procession lay dead, an awful pilgrimage of corpses stretching as far as the eye could see.

The Whispering Blade rasped in delight as the Bloodletter sheathed it once more.

Errol stared out across the bodies.

"We did this," the Bloodletter said.

"We did this," Errol repeated.

"And, no doubt, we'll do it again."

He took the boy's hand—gently—and together they walked along the trail of dead bodies. The Bloodletter could not help but notice that some of the men and women had died with expressions of happiness and love upon their faces. Soon, he turned away from the corpses and walked south, unsure of his destination other than—

Somewhere else.

"Sing us a song," the Bloodletter said to the boy.

To his surprise, the boy did.

ABOUT THE AUTHOR

CULLEN BUNN writes graphic novels such as *THE SIXTH GUN, HARROW COUNTY, BASILISK, THE GHOUL NEXT DOORS, DEADPOOL KILLS THE MARVEL UNIVERSE,* and *UNCANNY X-MEN.*